PULSE

LYDIA KWA

PULSE

KEY PORTER BOOKS

Library and Archives Canada Cataloguing in Publication

Kwa, Lydia, 1959–
        Pulse: a novel / Lydia Kwa.

ISBN 978-1-55470-259-6

        I. Title.

PS8571.W3P84 2010   C813'.54   C2009-905842-1

ONTARIO ARTS COUNCIL
CONSEIL DES ARTS DE L'ONTARIO

The publisher gratefully acknowledges the support of the Canada Council for the Arts and the Ontario Arts Council for its publishing program. We acknowledge the support of the Government of Ontario through the Ontario Media Development Corporation's Ontario Book Initiative.

We acknowledge the financial support of the Government of Canada through the Book Publishing Industry Development Program (BPIDP) for our publishing activities.

Key Porter Books Limited
Six Adelaide Street East, Tenth Floor
Toronto, Ontario
Canada M5C 1H6

www.keyporter.com

Text design: Sonya V. Thursby
Electronic formatting: Marijke Friesen

Printed and bound in Canada

10 11 12 13 5 4 3 2 1

For Joan Pillay and Joan Hollenberg
Two Graces

Moreover Jack sees that Jill herself knows what Jill thinks Jack knows, but that Jill does not realize she knows it.
—R. D. Laing, Knots

one 脈

Becoming possessed happens when you aren't watching. Sneaks up on you. You know without knowing. You mustn't argue with the seduction, the pull of the trance. When the moment arrives, something in you understands it's pointless to resist.

I was set off by the registered letter. When I recognized the handwriting on the envelope, my heart started to race.

I offered our postal carrier a thank-you smile, did my best to look normal as I signed for the letter. Possession is serious, and there's no need to share it with a stranger, especially the man from Canada Post. When he turned around and walked off, I frowned to myself.

How long has it been since I received a letter from Faridah? Far too long. When I get nervous, it helps to focus on minutiae. I can see from the stamped date on the envelope that the letter was processed at the Singapore Post Office on July 17. The *par avion* envelope with its border of red and blue flags boasts three stamps, all bearing an insignia on the top right-hand corner: the dark figure of a lion's head. Referring to the "Singa" in Singapore, city of lions. One stamp features a pair of blue turquoise fish. I've never seen such pretty fish. The other two stamps are a study in contrast: one a two-dollar stamp featuring a modern Singapore Bus Service double-decker bus with neither driver nor human passenger; the other, worth only thirty cents, of an electric tram with silhouettes of a driver and nine or ten passengers. I suppose that kind of tram would have been used in the early 1900s in Singapore, after a century of rickshaws and buffalo carts.

I can't risk reading the letter just yet. Have to wait until the end of the day, after seeing my patients. I stuff the envelope into the front pocket of my blue denim wraparound skirt.

I'm dressed for work, wearing a green linen blouse with this skirt, my favourite, a gift from Michelle, who found it at a thrift store on College. I like its clean lines. Minimalist yet funky. The large front pocket is smack in the middle of the skirt, right over my belly, covering my navel.

It's been ten minutes since the letter arrived, but my heart is still racing. I flex my left elbow and find the acupuncture point Heart 3, also known as *Shao Hai* or Lesser Sea. I press it for a few seconds, and then work on the same point on my right side. Then I press Heart 7, *Shen Men* or Spirit Gate, at the crease of each wrist, on the side of my pinky finger. This will bring down my anxiety.

Hiding behind partially drawn curtains in the living room, I watch a group of children playing outside: the two Vietnamese sisters with Hello Kitty barrettes in their hair, the lanky son of Iranian parents and the cute, wide-eyed Korean boy with the mini mohawk haircut, dressed in oversized jeans, a hand-me-down from his brother. Afternoon heat, shimmering along the edges, enters the pores of the children and suffuses them with glee. Sunlight animates the trio of plastic Canada Day flags, nestled among the cascades of blue lobelia in the planter box across the street.

Our stretch of old brick duplexes and townhouses on Baldwin between Huron and Beverley Streets in the area bordering Chinatown is only a block away from the trendy section east of Beverley. But it's a whole different world here, with its own sublime magic. Beneath the shabby deterioration exists an unconventional beauty. Unbeknownst to many, our street name, nicely transliterated into Chinese characters, means "Precious Cloud."

It's peaceful here. That's the way I like it. Many of our neighbours are immigrants. Some have been here more than thirty years. Others, like the Falun Gong people across the street, only months. Our neighbours are extraordinary people who have triumphed through quiet perseverance, unheralded in the larger social sphere. Some of them have had children only since arriving in Canada, sparing their offspring hardship they themselves endured in the old country. At least I'd like to think so, but I could be over-romanticizing.

I turn my head when I sense a slight movement from behind. Must be a mistake: Papa hasn't stirred from his seat. Sunlight filters through the gauze curtains and falls across his lap, razor-thin streaks of light running at an angle to the softer dusk blue waves of his corduroy pants.

Papa doesn't move much these days. The stroke occurred almost two and a half years ago, not long after Lunar New Year in February 2005. That would have been less than a week after we returned from our last trip to Singapore.

Ever since then, Mum and I feel as if we're living with a stranger. Since neither of us can claim to be mind readers, it's crude guesswork for us to imagine what Papa thinks or wants. During the day, if not prompted, he would sit for hours in his tan Ikea recliner, still as a Buddha. Who is this man with a vacant look and shell of a body? He has recovered some mobility in his right side, but he still requires help when walking, even with the support of a cane. What's worse is the loss of speech: although Papa will occasionally say a few words, he's no longer the man whose confident, booming voice once ruled our home in Singapore.

Oddly enough, music revives him. When we play his favourite songs, he starts to hum some of the lines and sometimes sings out loud. Twice a week, during rehab at St. Michael's, he waltzes gracefully across the floor with his occupational therapist. Debonair. That's when I believe my mother's stories of the charming man who romanced her. Funny yet touching to watch the old man doing the cha-cha with young Miss Turner to the tune of "Tea for Two."

When I was a student at U of T many years ago, I was taught to think of the brain as a conglomerate of site-specific functions. We read about Dr. Wilder Penfield's experiments at the Montreal Neurological Institute. Touch an electrode to a patient's raw, exposed brain and suddenly what seemed long lost is experienced freshly, as if it were happening in the present. Talk about magic. Talk about possession. All it took was a touch to the right spot. A simple and elegant concept. One spot for each memory, one spot for a particular kind of movement.

But Dr. Penfield couldn't settle for what he observed. Despite the compelling power of his own experiments, he wondered if the mind existed beyond the physical limits of the brain. When I read that about him, I was impressed. Now, that's a true scientist, someone who would remain open to alternative hypotheses. There must have been something Dr. Penfield felt, a hunch that came from being there, holding that electrode to the naked brain. So exposed, almost surreal. Even creepy.

If Dr. Penfield were here in this living room, touching an electrode to Papa's brain, I'm guessing that he would wonder about the mystery of my father's mind, whether Papa might recover and to what extent.

The news in Cantonese drifts in from the kitchen. I can tell that Mum is paying close attention because of the way she crunches crisp shrimp crackers. The rhythm of her snacking seems to track the tempo of the Toronto Chinese Radio announcer's voice. My mother uses her front incisors like percussion instruments. When the announcer mentions the recent killings by Chris Benoit, the professional wrestler known as The Canadian Crippler, the crunching stops momentarily, evidence of Mum's fascination with the case.

Our ancient clock chimes its tremulous melody, lagging a few minutes behind the news.

"Lunch ready," Mum calls out from the kitchen.

The twenty-something guy across the street revs the engine of his beat-up Yamaha motorcycle. Papa looks blankly at me, but his right hand moves a flicker, shifting perhaps an inch on the armrest. His arm, once muscular and tanned, is now limp and wasted, defined by large age spots and rubbery, wrinkled skin. He moves his mouth slightly. I lean closer to catch the sounds that he coaxes out with great effort.

"Scoo . . ." he begins. Then stops. Tries again, the hiss harder, more effortful, "Sc-sck-scoo . . ."

"You mean school? School's been out for a month now;

that's why the kids are playing outside at this time of day."

He blinks once, keeping his eyelids shut a little longer. That's his way of saying no.

He tries again, this time whispering, "No car."

It was a familiar mantra we lived with in Singapore: *We have no car*.

"Scooter?"

He blinks twice for a definite yes. Maybe the sound of the Yamaha awakened a memory in him. Those early days when he used to ride a Vespa. Who knows? Maybe even Papa, in his silent state, is possessed by the past.

AFTER slurping briskly through my bowl of rice noodle soup topped with fish balls and shrimp dumplings, I run into the washroom to brush my teeth. Check my face. I'm constantly told I don't look my age, whatever that means. Maybe it's the good hair-dye job. I think it means that people don't want to believe they can't deduce age from physical appearance, or that mortal decline isn't merely a tangible phenomenon.

I turned forty-eight recently. June 6, to be exact. That makes me as old as modern Singapore. After all, I was born that momentous day in 1959 when the People's Action Party government, under Lee Kuan Yew, began to run the country, independent of British rule. Even though the country remained part of the Federation of Malaya until 1965, the PAP under Prime Minister Lee took over the running of the island six years earlier, on the very day I appeared out of my mother's womb, two hours ahead of the government. To have one's existential debut coincide with the emergence of the country's self-government—I couldn't help but grow up believing that my fate could never be severed completely from Singapore's.

Every time I look at my reflection, I swear I can see my maternal grandmother Mah-Mah. I have her eyes. I remember the way she looked on a lazy afternoon in my grandfather's Chinese medicinal shop, Cosmic Pulse, as if her eyes were exploring another realm. Cosmic Pulse was my whole life until Papa decided our family needed to immigrate to Canada, in 1979.

My grandfather Kong-Kong had passed away in January 1978, leaving Cosmic Pulse in Mah-Mah's hands. She relied on Mum and my uncle to run the business until Papa changed all that.

I mustn't get too nostalgic. Too much pain to be had.

Check the time instead. It's 12:40 as I leave the house. I cross the street and pass the Benjamin Moore store on the corner, go by First Baptist Church on Huron. The sound of mah-jong chips being shuffled on tables drifts out from the two Chinese organizations near the corner of Dundas. I pop in to the Ten Ren store to get a taro milk bubble tea before I head toward Spadina.

Dundas is noisy, thick with the sounds of Toishan, Cantonese, Mandarin, Tagalog and an occasional flurry of Vietnamese. Cantopop spills from the store selling pirated

DVDS. I glance at the display screen just inside. It's Anita Mui performing "Bad Girl."

A few more blocks south, past the twenty-four-hour Asian Farm at Grange, then China City Supermarket before I reach the teashop downstairs from my clinic.

"Hey, Dr. Chia! Why don't you come in for some herbal tea? *Yit hei, tai duo yit hei.* You work too hard!" shouts Mrs. Kong from the back of the store.

She's right. Too much heat in my system. I nod in polite acknowledgement. "Sorry, no time right now. Another day!" Then I take the short flight of stairs adjacent to the shop, up to my clinic on the first floor.

Once inside, I open the three windows, one in the small waiting room and two in the treatment room. Take a few deep breaths. The smell of fresh towels lightly scented with lavender competes with the telling scent of yesterday's moxibustion treatments.

I switch on the fan in the treatment room, making sure to aim it away from the table. Then the quick check, an automatic set of habits I've performed for over twenty years. Stainless steel needles wait to be liberated from their sealed paper envelopes. Cotton balls in the glass jar. Cones of moxa, rolled late last night before I left the clinic. Lined up on the square plate like soldiers in Qin Shi Huangdi's army. I sigh with pleasure at the sight of my army of moxa, the tiny cones of wormwood that I burn on patients' skin to unblock channels of energy.

Back in the waiting room, I sit down at the rosewood desk and flip open my appointment book. The LED clock shows 12:55. First client, 2:00 p.m. Even when I don't have much to do, I come early just so I have some time to myself. There's a feeling of privacy in my clinic that I don't get at home.

Just behind me are two charts, drawings of the female and male bodies, depicting the hundreds of acupuncture points. These charts embody the principles I embrace. The Chinese character for "needle" is *zhen*: the radical for "gold" on the left side, and a symbol on the right that looks like a cross, or an arrow piercing a target. Shamans in the Shang dynasty used needles along with oracle bones to placate the anger of the spirits, thereby restoring harmony between the living and the dead.

I take the letter out of my skirt pocket, feeling momentarily tempted, but quickly slip it to the back of my appointment book. The past is sometimes so present. I was such a bitter young woman when I left Singapore. I feel tears come to my eyes. *Can't indulge, not now.*

From my position behind my rosewood desk, I stare out at the large mall across from me, then farther south to the large old buildings and the sign that announces CHARISMA FURS.

Not far from my clinic is the place where I experienced acupuncture for the first time. I was in my final year at U of T, completing a major in biology, with a minor in psychology. Just before Thanksgiving, I began to suffer frequent recurring nightmares, from which I would awaken confused and terrified. Alone in a dark room, lying on a bed with white sheets, I felt a heavy force push down on my whole being. The bed and I would fall through a deep shaft, toward the centre of the earth. I struggled to free myself, unable to move or speak.

While in the dream, I tried to convince myself that I was merely dreaming and therefore had no reason to be frightened, but some other logic in me insisted that I had to escape the dream in order to survive. I needed to make a sound, to cry out or scream, because I believed that speech would free the rest of my body and allow me to break the paralysis.

The nightmare kept returning. The world of sleep felt ominous.

Music became my refuge. During sleep-deprived days, hauling myself from class to class, my mind turned to scenes from *The Hunger*. I kept myself fuelled listening to "Bela Lugosi's Dead." All through the nights in the genetics lab at Ramsay Wright, as I carefully crossed *Drosophila* flies from F1 generations, watching their progeny and noting down the characteristics, I heard the refrain of "Undead, undead, undead" echo through my loneliness. Walking home at 2:00 a.m., I would sing David Bowie: "Hunt you to the ground they will, mannequins with kill appeal."

The more honest the lyrics about the threat of harm from other humans, the more reassured I felt. I wasn't the only one afflicted by a prolonged episode of possession.

By the time winter solstice arrived, I was desperate for escape. One afternoon, while trudging through the snow-caked streets of Chinatown, I spotted a sign in the second-floor window of a shop on Huron. Those few lines in English, a translation of Lao Tzu, startled me:

Mere existing
Sheer dead weight
Only in emptiness does life begin.

Even though I didn't have the slightest understanding of what those lines meant, there was something both disturbing and appealing about the notion that emptiness was a prerequisite for becoming alive. There were a few thousand years between Lao Tzu and David Bowie, between Taoism and punk rock, but it wasn't hard for me to imagine the old sage dressed in black in a goth music video, singing those lines.

What did emptiness mean? The saying seemed to imply that inanimate objects didn't possess this quality. *Well*, I thought, *a person could be dead while alive*. Did emptiness have something to do with the ability to move, to change oneself?

I felt dizzy with the effort of trying to make sense of this riddle, and shut my eyes tightly. It didn't take long before I saw bats hanging down from the ceilings of dank caves—thousands of them, their eyes looking out into the darkness. Searching for Dracula, or Bowie, or some representative from the undead that could inform about death, dead weight and the possibility of redemption.

"What the heck," I mumbled. I opened my eyes and ran up the stairs to the herbal shop. Dr. Ting peered carefully at me, then asked many questions. Next, she told me to stick out my tongue so she could study the signs of imbalances showing up there. Last, she took my pulses on both wrists. She pronounced the problem as "rising fire in the heart" and inserted that first needle into the side of my wrist below my left pinky.

It's impossible to capture precisely what happened. When the needle entered the side of my wrist, an arrow of sensation penetrated further, deep below the skin. It was an electrifying leap that startled me. I breathed a huge sigh of relief without understanding why. Everything around me—the chairs and books, the glass cabinets, even Dr. Ting's white coat—seemed to settle more easily within my awareness, as if the world was no longer so threatening that it had to be kept outside.

That was my first encounter with Heart 7: *Shen Men*, Spirit Gate. That magic needle summoned my spirit back and calmed my mind. It was inexplicably powerful.

Five sessions later, my nightmares disappeared completely. I've never had them since. I decided not to pursue graduate studies in biology and instead switched to acupuncture, following in my grandfather's footsteps as a traditional healer.

THE afternoon passes quickly as I see three patients one after the other. During a half-hour break at 5:30, I run to the nearest bakery to buy a steamed chicken bun. Then two more patients, the last appointment being Michelle's father.

Mr. Woo is seventy-eight, three years older than my father, though he seems much younger. He jokes a lot, eyes glimmering with mirth, and walks with a light step. He likes to take my last appointment of the day at 7:30 because he says it ensures a good night's sleep.

On the treatment table, he relaxes completely, with his eyes shut. Unlike my father, Mr. Woo doesn't mind needles. Besides being my girlfriend's father, he's also my taiji teacher. He teaches taiji and qigong at the neighbourhood community centre. During root canal surgery last month, he didn't need either anaesthesia or acupuncture. That's what I call impressive.

Around the time of his wife's passing, five years ago, his pulses indicated a weakening of the lungs due to grief. He came down with a bad case of the flu and was at risk of developing pneumonia. But he recovered and has remained remarkably at peace.

"Watching soccer lately?" he asks, with a slight smile on his face, eyes still closed.

"No ..."

"You and Michelle crazy watching World Cup last year."

I laugh. He likes to tease. It's really his daughter who's soccer mad.

"I only went crazy during the last game."

"Who can stay calm watching World Cup? Even I got excited. What was his name, that man lost temper? Start with Z."

"Zidane."

"Yeah, not enough yin. Need do qigong. Can help a lot."

"Are you sure that wasn't you in *Pushing Hands*?"

He smiles. I know he recognizes the reference to Ang Lee's movie about a taiji teacher. I'm guessing he takes it as a compliment. I put in needles to nourish his kidney energy, needles in the heels of both feet, and needles to disperse heat from his liver meridian—acupuncture points just on the inside of his knees, near the crease. I leave him for twenty minutes, with the needles in him, while I dart into the waiting room. While writing down some notes in Mr. Woo's file, I glance at Faridah's letter waiting for me at the back of my appointment book.

When I touch Mr. Woo on his arm to indicate we're done, his eyelids flutter open with a gentle grace. After he's left the clinic, I lock the front door and smile to myself. Such a pleasure treating him.

When the sheets and towels are finally in the dryer, I sit down with a cup of ginger tea and pull out the envelope. I tear it open carefully, along the short edge, wanting to spare the stamps. Inside, there's only a single sheet of paper, as fine and delicate as skin.

Faridah's handwriting remains distinctive, her letters shaped as if they belong to a long-extinct language. Unafraid to show flourish. The ink is smudged in a few places.

Dear Nat,

I've struggled countless times over the past week with whether or not to write to you. But I have to, need to.

Look, I don't want you to misunderstand my motivation. True, I had to choose a direction that took me farther away from you, but I've never veered from my feelings of affection for you, nor have I ever doubted that you were devoted to our friendship. I'm sorry it's come to this.

I'm reaching out to you during an impossibly trying time. I feel adrift. We have no idea just how long we still have to enjoy this life.

What an odd and serious beginning. I force myself to stop reading, to pause for a few deep breaths. She still has a way with words. Used to make me feel breathless just listening to her argue with Miss Rajah in class. Dramatic and assertive. That girl I had fallen in love with.

My attention drifts outside, drawn by the mix of voices and traffic on Spadina. Just past 8:30 p.m., but Chinatown still bustles with diners and shoppers. A Falun Gong message from loudspeakers up the street penetrates my consciousness. A few moments later, I resume reading the letter.

How could we have suspected? What's the meaning of this? Our beloved Selim is gone, taken from us. He's dead, Natalie. He killed himself. I was the one who found him hanging from the ceiling in his room. He had rigged up ropes from the overhead light fixtures.

The delicate paper quivers in my hand.

I can't bear to repeat all the details. What words could adequately convey the extent of our loss?

I imagine her at the desk, struggling to write these words down. The paper so thin that, if she had not been careful, it would have been ripped by the force of her handwriting. The next few lines mention the funeral, which occurred already, on the 20th of July, five days ago. But there will be a memorial service in two weeks.

Our son's death has devastated our family. Christina is frightened now of sleeping in her room, which is next to his. She thinks she can hear her brother's voice teasing her late at night.

The police are investigating, as a matter of course, to rule out foul play.

But what a phrase! "Foul play."

I've taken time off work, but Adam can't afford to break down. The teachers and students need him.

I find myself panicking about some unresolved issues.
This is also why I'm writing to you. Taking a risk, per-
haps asking too much. I wish you could return to Singa-
pore in time for the memorial. It's a need that I can't
rationalize away, Natalie. There still exists an ache for
what we lost, which, I realize, we can never recover.

There the letter ends, as abruptly as it began. She signs her name, the large flowery "F" and the bold upward tail to the "h" trailing off to the right, as if she never wants to be stopped or held back. That was what she was like, all fiery and rebellious. Her handwriting is as elegant as ever. Devastating news conveyed with a steady hand, yet the words on the page are smudged by tears.

Can't believe it. Selim dead? I fold the letter precisely along the same creased lines. My hands are still trembling.

The neon lights outside glare at me as I start to cry. A hollow sensation comes over me, spreads from the centre of my torso out toward my arms and legs. I lose track of time.

When I finally pause to wipe my tears away, I decide to check my pulses.

I rest my left hand on the small cushion on my desk and position the index, middle and ring fingers of my other hand along the radial artery on the wrist, taking pulses the way I've been accustomed to doing as a Traditional Chinese Medicine acupuncturist. I close my eyes to concentrate better. The index finger on the *cun* position detects patterns from the heart and small intestine meridians; the middle finger on the *guan* position, from the liver and gallbladder meridians; the ring finger on the *chi* position, from the right kidney and bladder meridians. I begin with the first reading, using a moderate pressure of the fingers, what we call "searching"; next, I apply a firmer pressure for the second reading, termed "pressing." Last, I lift my three fingers up for a light touch, called "touching." Then I take pulses on the other wrist, fingers on the same positions, which indicate patterns of the lung and large intestine meridians, spleen and stomach meridians, the left kidney meridian and the adrenal system.

There are no detectable pulses on both wrists at the light and medium levels of pressure; only when I probe more firmly—at the "pressing" level—can I pick up a faint pulse through my ring fingers placed at the *chi* point on both wrists. The quality of the pulses confirms it: I'm showing the signs of someone in shock, the kidneys and adrenal glands most affected by the news about Selim.

I take a slow, deep breath. *Try to calm yourself.*

MY MIND is caught in a swirl of questions as I walk down Spadina, heading home.

I used to think that possession was a rare dramatic occurrence, the province of temple mediums.

I'm not a temple medium, but I know what it's like to feel overcome by the force of memories, to feel disoriented and lost, if only temporarily. I shelter my left hand inside the front pocket of my skirt, cradling the letter as I try to focus on the surroundings.

Many of my favourite eating haunts have disappeared, the places I used to frequent after midnight while I was studying at U of T. Delectable displays of barbecued ducks hanging in the window don't have the same power of reassurance for me tonight. A strip of sky is pale yellow behind the storefronts on the west side of the wide avenue, light failing under the weight of dark mauve. Each neon sign is an afterthought against darkness.

I pause in front of the LCBO before I turn onto Baldwin. Wish I could push away the feelings welling up inside me. I count thirteen whites and four people of colour going in or out of the liquor store. Ridiculous habit, but at least it distracts.

When I've had enough, I resume my walk home. By the time I reach our townhouse, the living room is sheathed in darkness, the curtains fully drawn. But I catch a glimmer of light filtering out from the kitchen into our hallway. I don't feel like rushing inside. I stand there, in the cool night air, listening to the silence of the street, shivering as sadness takes hold of me.

two 脈

Faridah periodically shared details of Selim's life over the years. Following the end of our relationship in 1975, we had hardly had any contact, even before I left Singapore.

The joy of having Selim, in 1980, seemed to open her up once again. She wrote me a card here and there, enclosing photos of the family as the years progressed. Sometimes I would reciprocate, usually sending a postcard with a Toronto theme, but I would not offer anything too revealing about my life. I had turned a corner, and I found myself unable to be as open with Faridah as I once was.

I equated Selim's birth with the end of silence between Faridah and me, though it was not enough to overcome the irreparable rift between us.

Gabriel Tat Meng Selim Khoo was given several names to reflect his mixed heritage. Upon finishing his bachelor's degree at the National University of Singapore, he wanted to use his Malay name instead of his English one. He insisted that family and close friends call him Selim. He said he was tired of being an angel of God. It was his father, Adam, who had given him the name Gabriel, and Adam's parents who came up with the Chinese names, but it was Faridah's father, Osman, who had provided the name Selim, meaning "peace," similar to the Hebrew variant "shalom." Although his grandfather identified himself as Malay, he didn't use the popular Malay spelling, "Salim." Uncle Osman picked the name and that particular spelling to reflect the connection to their Arabic lineage—albeit distant—tracing their history back to the Ottoman Empire.

On his identity card, Selim was listed as Chinese, in accordance with Adam's ethnicity. But that's part of the inconsistency. Adam is really a Baba, a male of mixed Malay and Chinese heritage. But neither Babas nor Nonyas would be acknowledged on their identity cards. I knew from Faridah that Adam was infuriated by his son's decision to privilege his Malay name over his Christian one. He took it as a personal insult.

After doing their national service, Selim and his boyhood friend Philip went to university, then joined the police force. Faridah was unhappy with Selim's decision to become a policeman. She had wanted him to continue his studies, maybe even go abroad. Adam's reaction had been quite the opposite.

I didn't know Selim well for most of his life. Most of what I knew, I learned from Faridah. But a visit to Singapore in February 2005 changed all that.

MY PARENTS and I had returned to see some relatives and friends for Chinese New Year. This was about a week before Papa suffered his stroke.

On day two of the Year of the Rooster, the Khoo family had a beach picnic at Marine Parade, occupying one of the open-air gazebos. They—along with a few thousand others—took advantage of the public holidays to camp out facing the ocean.

Selim had been a policeman for barely a year. Both of Faridah's parents were there: Uncle Osman was by then a shrunken version of the man I had known in my youth, but he was holding court in his beach chair, chatting about the good old days at *Utusan Melayu*, while Aunty Sylvia, immaculate in her *sarong kebaya*, busied herself with putting out the *kueh* desserts and savoury snacks. Adam's father had passed away a long time before, but his mother was still alive, and sat meekly on the stone bench, looking overwhelmed by the crowd of guests.

I felt uncomfortable when I noticed the various ways the family addressed Selim. Uncle Osman and Aunty Sylvia spoke to their grandson far more than to their granddaughter Christina, Selim's younger sister. They called him Selim with a certain gleam of approval in their eyes. I could understand why Uncle Osman would behave like that, given what I knew about him, but I was surprised at Aunty's manner. After all, she was Nonya, a product of intermarriage between a Chinese man and a Malay woman. I wouldn't have expected her to be biased toward the use of the Malay name, but then again, she was Uncle Osman's wife and probably felt a need to side with him.

I also witnessed the palpable anger coming from Adam, his sour expression every time he heard his in-laws use his son's Malay name. It was one thing to hear about that anger second-hand from Faridah, but another thing to witness it myself. Adam persisted in calling his son Gabriel, and Selim ignored him. Meanwhile, Christina lay back on a mat with her iPod headphones on, tuning everyone out. If it weren't for the fact that she was sighing a lot, I wouldn't have guessed that the tension between her father and brother got to her.

It was disconcerting to witness the tension between Selim and his father. I was an outsider, awkwardly witnessing a family drama that I had only the most superficial knowledge of. I had spent most of my teenage years being best friends with Faridah, and saw a lot of Uncle Osman and Aunty Sylvia, since I often visited their home. But then, they had no idea just how close Faridah and I had become. They had no idea we were lovers.

In the years following my estrangement from Faridah, Adam became the focus of Uncle Osman and Aunty Sylvia's concern. He was the boyfriend, so they were happy about that. He wasn't pure Chinese, but was a third-generation Baba of parents who were also hybrids. Although Aunty Sylvia approved of him, I think Uncle Osman had hoped that Faridah would choose a Malay man. I heard about Uncle Osman's ambivalence through the grapevine. I'm guessing he would have been upset that Faridah got pregnant before marriage. Maybe that was why he hadn't been entirely enthusiastic. But he warmed up to his son-in-law, especially after Selim was born.

At the Chinese New Year beach picnic in 2005, I was uncomfortable around Adam. After all, he had married the one I loved. The discomfort wasn't one way, either. I often noticed Adam glancing at me surreptitiously. I felt self-conscious, made sure I stayed a safe distance from Faridah and refrained from showing any signs of affection. It was hard to do. My friend, so vivacious and lovely, was laughing a lot and moving about with a sensual confidence.

For most of that afternoon, Selim sat on the straw mat next to Christina, trying to draw her out from her musical bubble. He seemed to enjoy teasing his younger sister, and she didn't seem to mind. He ate heartily, with loud slurps of appreciation. I watched him eat, amused by his unrestrained enjoyment of food. Not quite twenty-five at the time and already so confident. He wasn't worried about showing hunger as the shameless instinct that it is.

I was thinking how much Selim looked like Faridah: lean build, large black eyes, strongly sensuous mouth. It pleased yet pained me to watch him. It was as if I had been transported back to my young teenage self again.

Facing Selim on the mat was a handsome, dark-skinned Tamil man. I guessed he was Philip. He occasionally got up to fill his plate with more food, but aside from that, he hardly socialized with others. He smiled shyly at me a few times, but we only made small talk about the food being delicious. Like me, Philip hovered at the edge of the family constellation. He acted as if he was comfortable with everyone, but he was constantly averting his gaze, choosing to look away into the distance, past people. I liked his eyes, though. I thought there was evidence of a rebellious spirit.

Toward the end of the picnic, I walked away from the gazebo and onto the sand, to look out at the ocean. I was tired of noticing people's discomfort with one another. Selim came to join me, standing close.

It was an odd moment. We didn't speak for quite a while, but watched the ocean together. It felt nice to have his company. But feelings associated with Faridah arose inside me, emotions that I thought had long since disappeared. A surge of desire, as well as sadness over a long-lost dream.

Selim finally turned his whole body to face me. He touched me gently on my shoulder, then leaned closer and spoke softly. "I know who you are. You needn't hide it, Cosmic Pulse."

A shudder went down the back of my neck. His tone of voice, the way he so deliberately phrased it. I knew he wasn't referring to the name of my grandfather's shop. But how could he have known about my virtual identity?

He saw the fear in my eyes and quickly added, "No need to worry; your secret is safe with me. Let's talk soon."

Selim called me the next morning, my last day before returning to Toronto. He wanted to meet up. We needed an unhurried chat, he said, to really catch up on all those lost years while I was away in Canada. I was impressed by his insistence. We agreed to meet at Boat Quay that evening.

I SAT waiting next to Botero's *Bird* in front of the UOB towers, on one of the marble cube stools at the water's edge. The pronounced sea smell of the Singapore River rose up to my nostrils as the waves hit the mossy stone steps of Boat Quay. Across the river, slightly west of the Asian Civilizations Museum, was the spot where Raffles is presumed to have landed on the island. The sharply delineated eye of a *tongkang* puttered by on the water. I stared at the building that now housed the museum, trying to remember what it used to be called.

"Hey." Selim had approached from behind me.

I felt the hairs on my neck rise up as I turned around. He looked tired, shadows under his eyes. He was dressed in a dark green polo shirt and a pair of jeans that flattered his long, lean legs.

"Let's go have a beer," he suggested.

We walked west toward the strip of bars and restaurants at the farther end of the quay. The setting sun imparted an orange brilliance to the scene. The darkening skyscrapers of the new Singapore loomed over us, monumental.

We decided on Harry's Bar, chose a table at the water's edge. After the waitress brought us our beers, Selim lit a cigarette and offered me his pack of Marlboro's.

"No thanks, don't smoke."

"Oh yeah, acupuncturist. Very healthy lifestyle. Like your grandfather, right or not? What, you don't like my accent?"

I smiled anxiously at his performance. He was deliberately putting on a heavy Singlish accent, but it wasn't his accent that unnerved me. I felt intimidated because, only the day before, he had alluded to my identity as Cosmic Pulse.

"Did you know that not far from here was the area my maternal great-great-grandparents settled?"

"No, I didn't know that."

"I feel so distant from my Malay side, you know. Mom hardly talks about that history these days. She used to."

I frowned, unsure of Selim's meaning. His voice was definitely tense, but was he sad or disapproving?

"Really? I'm surprised."

"Who knows why." He shrugged. "I mean, she used to

tell me more stories when I was a kid. Maybe there's too much regret or…" He looked away, shifting uneasily in his chair.

"Well, your mom and I grew up during a time when Singapore was going through a lot of political change. There was all that tension between the Chinese and Malays. And the race riots…"

I thought of the time Papa and I narrowly escaped being harmed in July 1964. We were in Geylang Serai when his scooter stalled on a dirt road next to a field of lallang grass. We spotted a gang of Malay men with parangs approaching us from the far side of the field. We were saved when a lorry drove by and blocked the path between the men and us, allowing Papa to finally start up his Vespa and drive away.

"*One united people, regardless of race, language or religion,*" he responded, quoting from Singapore's National Pledge. "Sounds wonderful, but the reality is that people have become quite unsettled since 9/11."

"You mean people have become more nervous around Muslims?"

"In general, yes. There's an underlying tension that wasn't there before 9/11, with the exception of those race riots in '64, of course. It's gotten worse since the arrests of those guys from Jemaah Islamiah in 2001 and 2002. That's why the government has been encouraging Muslims to devote themselves to what is positive and non-violent in their religion."

"Hope it works."

"Unlike your generation, it's not simply a question of race anymore. Especially when there's more and more of us in Singapore who are racially mixed. It's all about religion. Christianity against Islam."

I shuddered at Selim's blunt, dramatic pronouncement. How dark the world had become. "Violence is bred in the mind," I muttered, feeling uneasy at the sombreness of our conversation.

"It's all in our minds, isn't it? Which side we're on."

"Or even the notion of sides."

"You know what? I'm sick and tired of the way things don't get dealt with honestly. Sometimes we humans act as if difficult problems will disappear as long as we don't talk about them. But it takes a lot more energy to deny truth. I want to face things. Become a responsible, honest citizen who contributes positively to society. Too many of my peers care only about money and wasting it. I don't have time for that. I want to devote myself to some worthy pursuits. That's partly why I chose to use the name Selim."

"Because it means 'peace'?"

"Yes. I want that. To be peaceful, peacemaking."

I smiled, hearing Selim's words. I thought of my father praying to God while he frantically tried to get his scooter started on that dirt road in Geylang Serai. Papa said out loud that he would dedicate my life to Him if we survived that encounter. It seemed to me that there was a vast, irreconcilable difference between Papa's "dedication" and the kind of devotion Selim was talking about. He sounded quite resolved to take responsibility for his choices. No God would need to intervene on his behalf.

Selim inhaled deeply from his cigarette and continued, "Enough of that. On to an entirely different topic." He leaned across the table and whispered, "Do you think there's such a thing as 'good pain'?"

I frowned. "What?"

"That pain isn't always a bad thing."

I felt uncomfortable, didn't want to answer.

He noticed. "One person's pain is another's pleasure, right?" he quipped, laughing. Then he continued, "Hey, like I told you yesterday at our silly Marine Parade picnic, there's no need for concern." He unbuttoned the front left pocket of his shirt and took out a ballpoint pen. He scribbled hastily on the back of a Tiger Beer paper coaster, then pushed it toward me. On it were the words "Benkulen Bound." A username I recognized from the Kinbaku online chat room.

I took a few slow breaths, trying to take in this incredible revelation. "Oh God, so you're . . . ?"

"Yes, I'm Benkulen Bound."

"But how did you know I was Cosmic Pulse?"

"My mother told me the name of your grandfather's herbal medicine shop a long time ago. Like I said, she used to regale me with stories about her past. Which included things about you. So that's how I knew. When I went to the chat room, I figured Cosmic Pulse had to be you. Especially when you went on and on about healing one's spirit through binding the body!"

I blushed. He must have thought I was pretty tame. Benkulen Bound, after all, had hard-core notions about bondage.

"Stunned, aren't you? As they say, *a small world*."

"What a crazy coincidence, both of us interested in Kinbaku."

"But with two opposite approaches to the rope."

I nodded. When I first began practising the Kinbaku rope techniques, I checked out the website and decided to join the online chat room so that I could exchange ideas with others interested in this art of Japanese erotic bondage. As I found out soon enough, people in the chat room were divided. Benkulen Bound was the most adamant among the online participants that pain was essential to Kinbaku. Benkulen Bound insisted we must not get "too soft" in our approach. It was clear that he was a gay man who used Kinbaku rope techniques within a Western BDSM practice. He identified himself as a slave, or bottom, and he definitely liked to play it risky.

Others of us in the chat room took a different position. As Cosmic Pulse, I argued that binding the body with rope allowed us to transform our fears and develop trust; in addition, it was an erotic practice that not only gave pleasure in the moment, but also allowed further satisfaction after the fact, with the experience of touching or viewing the temporary markings left by the rope on the body.

I stared out across the Singapore River, mesmerized by the bursts of light reflected on the water from the kerosene lamplights of the tugboats and *tongkangs*. I recalled my brief history in the chat room. As the *nawashi*, the one who binds, I see my role as one of servicing my partner. I don't even like to think of the one I bind as my bottom, or slave. I soon stopped participating in the online chats. I felt I knew enough by that time, and I was taking the practice in a direction I wanted.

"Why are you revealing yourself to me now?"

"It's a chance I can't miss." His eyes met mine. Penetratingly. He gestured with the cigarette in his left hand, pointing in the direction of the river, yet he seemed to hint at some place past it.

"Like I said, one person's pain is another's pleasure."

"A double entendre. How clever."

He grinned widely. "You haven't answered my question about good pain and bad pain."

"I'm not sure if I can answer it." I felt sad. I didn't know why my ex-lover's son needed to be so candid about his need for pain.

He shrugged with resignation, then continued, "Did my mom ever tell you that we're distantly related to Munshi Abdullah, the famous tutor and interpreter for Sir Stamford Raffles? That's what gave me the idea to call myself Benkulen Bound. Smart, huh?"

Raffles' views were instrumental in developing the myth of Malay backwardness, so much so that for most of the nineteenth century, his arguments about the so-called decay of Malay society were implicitly accepted by Europeans. Munshi Abdullah may have liked a lot of Raffles' ideas, but not the ones about the laziness of Malays.

"I know about your family connection to Munshi Abdullah. Your grandfather talked about it when I used to visit your mother at their place." Of course Uncle Osman was proud to be a descendant; Munshi Abdullah was famous not only because he worked for Raffles, but also because he wrote an extensive account of life in the East Indies, the *Hikayat Abdullah*.

His eyes gleamed. "You know how devoted Grandpa Osman was in advocating for Malay rights." He blew a whiff of smoke directly at me.

"Does that have something to do with you using your middle name?"

"I wanted to shake things up. I don't like being taken for granted. Yeah ... that's partly the reason."

"It's a lovely name."

"So what if my father doesn't approve? I don't care."

But his quivering lower lip tells a different story, I thought.

I had seen past his bravura. And he knew it. He lowered his voice. "Care about peace. Like a little bit of pain on the side. Aren't I full of contradictions, huh?" He turned away, but I could see tears welling up in his eyes.

I reached out and touched his hand lightly. "Hey, what's going on?"

He withdrew his hand abruptly, flinching as if he had

been slapped. "Is there a God out there? And will this . . . this . . . Supreme Being punish someone who hates his father?"

"I don't know." I swallowed hard, thrown off by the blunt confession.

"No matter what I do, he never seems to be happy with it." His voice cracked.

"But . . ." I struggled to find the words. "It's not your fault."

"What? What's not my fault?" His jaw tensed suddenly and he sat up, leaning his elbows on the table.

"Your father's negative attitude—whatever you want to call it."

I felt a dull ache in my chest, a burden of memory that asserted itself yet again. There was a part of me that wanted to get up from the chair and run. Far away from this raw, intense exposure. Wasn't life hard enough? Did we need to keep worrying the wound? Again and again?

When Selim spoke again, his voice had regained a steady, firm tone. "Haven't you ever wanted to risk?"

"Risk what?"

"Haven't you ever wanted to see what it's like to be the one bound? Not knowing what to expect next. I know you're not into pain, but what about surrendering control?"

"Not prepared to risk like that. You're Benkulen Bound, not me."

"Really? So you've never surrendered to anyone, then?"

"No, never!"

But he knew that I was lying.

"You know, many people who are in control or in positions of great responsibility in their public lives gravitate toward being in the so-called submissive position in a bondage scene. I'm a prime example of this. It gives me a chance to experience surrender. Relinquish control. That's not so different from what you said about overcoming fears and developing trust."

"Yeah, okay. And so . . ."

"You should let yourself take a turn in the submissive position sometime."

"I like exercising power in all aspects of my life."

"You know that being a submissive doesn't mean not having power."

I felt unnerved by his intelligence. He wasn't going to let me off so easy. But I didn't want to acknowledge what he was saying. It felt far too dangerous and vulnerable.

"I like control over needles, over my business, over my lovers. I don't have a passive side that requires rescuing. Besides, I hate these stupid distinctions anyway: dominant, submissive. They're artificial. It's not just an action that defines what a person is, it's one's internal state of mind."

He threw up his hands and laughed. "Well, okay. But hey, at the end of the day, actions speak louder, huh? Never mind, I'll surrender my position. Just because. I'm not the one with the hang-up about surrendering."

I smiled and shrugged my shoulders. "I agree, talk is talk. Words are cheap these days. Yeah, so I'm a disillusioned middle-aged dyke. What else is new? People never completely obey theories. Not even their own. What do I know? Maybe I'm fooling myself."

"That may make you more honest than someone who insists on their honesty."

I watched the night revellers pass by, looking for a place to have a drink or a meal. People looking for a good time, or to at least stave off their feelings of loneliness. A man and a woman strolled by, arms entwined, heading toward Clarke Quay, looking blissed out.

"I wouldn't be surprised if you changed your mind one day. Mark my words." He raised his index finger at me in a mock gesture of sternness. He looked like he was trying to impersonate a teacher.

"Such an archaic phrase: 'mark my words.' Did you pick it up from your father?"

"Yeah, I suppose . . . my father uses it a lot at school." The muscle along the left side of his jaw twitched suddenly.

I changed the topic. "Not many people think up usernames that connect to their ancestral heritage. I'm impressed by how you came up with yours."

"History is important. I'm only stating the obvious to you, Aunty Natalie. Besides, look who's talking: the person who named herself after her grandfather's shop. Eh, Cosmic Pulse?"

"Sure. But history would be boring without a bit of embellishment. Some may even argue that history itself is embellishment."

"Just like a good piece of fiction, right?" He chortled, his humour returning. Then he continued, "As for me, I prefer to investigate history. Learn from it."

"Not get stuck..."

"You bet. Hey, can I tell you something?"

"What?"

"My ambition."

I nodded, waiting eagerly.

"I want to eventually work in special investigations in the police."

"Really? Sounds interesting."

"That would be quite satisfying." Selim shifted his position, angling his body off to one side, and tapped the side of the table with the thumb and forefinger of his left hand. His gaze drifted past me, as if he were lost in thought. I kept quiet. After a few minutes, he said, "Nothing in life is a coincidence. Whatever we've inherited. From family or strangers. Whether we believe in Allah or the Christian God, whatever. Order and chaos, good and evil. Friend, enemy. Bloody dichotomies. We're all connected, unable to escape the impact we have on one another."

I looked down at the water. It was dark by this time, and the reflection of the lantern lights on the canopy flitted up to me, unheralded gems dancing on the surface of a dirty body of water. A beautiful moment could exist despite contamination. I tried to remember the young girl I had been, the one who had fallen in love.

It felt so pure then. For three years.

"We're constantly hungering for transcendence."

"What's that?" I heard him, but I wasn't sure what he was getting at. I shifted my glance away from the dark watery surface to refocus on Selim.

"Humans are constantly looking for a good time that will take us out of suffering. But it's all bullshit, anyway. It's love we hunger for, right? The unconditional kind. That's what will convince us we've transcended suffering."

The lyrics of a song rushed into my head, and I started to hum, "Love is the drug, got a hook on me . . . catch that buzz . . . the drug I'm thinking of . . . can't you see . . . love is the drug for me."

"Most definitely. Contaminated love—unlike the unconditional kind—comes with hooks, or maybe claws." He looked angry, judging from the fire in his eyes. "I refuse to take comfort in sentimental ideas, what I consider rather discomforting notions. Boring!"

"I hate being bored too."

"We share quite a few things in common, don't we? Including love for my mother."

I pursed my lips at this. He must know.

"Listen, can we keep in touch? There's so much more to talk about. I can't tell you how happy I was when I guessed that you were Cosmic Pulse. It isn't a coincidence that we're both into Kinbaku. I can't tell you everything all at once. I've got lots to ask you as well. The climate here...and me being in the police...I don't need to spell it out for you, do I?"

He finished his pint. Ordered another round for both of us. Then he lit a second cigarette and used his lighter to burn the coaster, letting the ashes collect in the no-name ashtray.

three 脈

I shiver. Either the temperature has dropped drastically in the thirty minutes I've been standing on Baldwin, or I'm feeling a chill from recalling my chat with Selim in February two and a half years ago. I rub my arms vigorously to warm up before I unlock the front door.

Entering the hallway, I make out the muted sound of the TV coming from the kitchen. Mum is intently watching one of her Cantonese serials with the volume turned down low, while a pork and turnip stew simmers on the stove. I recognize that look on Mum's face. She's in her nightly trance, eyes mesmerized by the drama.

"What's this show called?"

She doesn't answer me but instead waves to the pot and says, "Eat."

I join her with my bowl of food. On the screen, a sob-bing woman is ruining her mascara. An old black-and-white movie with scratchy, squiggly lines. I steal a glance at Mum. Her usual steely expression is softened by the melodrama. Soon she's crying without restraint, not both-ering to wipe away her tears. The heroine of the story is rooting in her handbag for her hankie when a handsome man enters the office.

"Hubbie's assistant," Mum informs me.

He's coming toward her. Moves confidently yet shows sensitivity. He wants her to know he isn't afraid to see her like this, but he knows she might get frightened if he moves too fast. As she turns away from him, he gently places his hands on her shoulders and says, "Don't be afraid." In Cantonese, of course.

I turn away momentarily to fixate instead on the halo-gen light glowing above the sink. Lighting devices are looking more and more like UFOs these days.

Somewhere, in another galactic system—or perhaps that fourth dimension Einstein told us was possible—all the feelings, all the memories that human beings across the ages couldn't accept or live with, are alive and thriving, never completely lost. I imagine all the yearning and mis-givings, the rage, even excessive sentiment, churning in a black hole of immense proportions.

I glance back at my mother, who remains entirely im-mersed in the melodrama. I've never met anyone who could match her capacity to become lost in make-believe worlds—worlds that grant her a much-needed solace.

I suppose it must have been that capacity that led her to not see some of the awful things happening in our family. She couldn't afford to know, could she? To admit to what she might know. Where did she put those memories and instincts?

I don't think it's a good time to tell Mum the news about Selim.

He wanted to contribute to peace for others, yet he craved pain in a Kinbaku scene. Not much more than half my age, yet he dared to be so bold and articulate about his contradictions. Was Selim able to achieve the peace he said he longed to embody?

I take a deep breath, smell the salty air of that elusive ocean along the east coast of Singapore, now flooding our Toronto kitchen with bittersweet memories. I try to watch the movie, but the feelings of unease well up inside, making it difficult for me to sit quietly. After about half an hour, I sneak away upstairs.

I MAKE sure my door is shut tight before I make the call. On the other end of the line, I hear the phone ring with that familiar pairing of two quick rings followed by a pause before the next pair of sounds. I count six rings.

"Hello?"

"Faridah, it's Natalie."

Silence. I can hear Faridah's breathing over the line.

The reception's so clear, it's as if she's in the same room, sitting next to me. When she finally speaks, her voice sounds almost disbelieving. "So you got my letter, then?"

"Earlier today. It's unbelievable. I'm very sorry . . ." I stop myself from saying more. I'm filled with a sense of my own uselessness. Words seem so facile.

I hear a sharp intake of air at her end, then another long pause.

"You could have emailed, saved your money."

"Did I catch you at a bad time?"

"Adam's in the living room, watching football. Can't talk long, but I appreciate your call. It's Saturday here, just past noon. We'll be heading out to the *kopi tiam* to eat as soon as the game is over."

"How are you?"

"Me? I don't know what to say. Police have no evidence to indicate that it's anything else but . . . but a suicide."

"How horrible. And for you to be the one to find him."

"There was music coming from his room. Nothing surprising about that. Too loud, as usual. I was going to tell him to turn down the volume. Knocked on his door. Didn't suspect anything, and then . . . barged in, all ready to scold him. And, and . . ." A stifled sob.

My guts start to churn, and a wave of nausea rises up in my throat. I turn my head away from the phone receiver and cover my mouth, fighting the urge to throw up.

She continues, "I keep telling myself I have to be strong, but I don't feel it. Can't work, don't want to do anything.

Except cry all the time."

"I don't know what to say."

"Why did he do it? And in that way? In our home? Why?"

Her voice is choked. Rage and grief spill out in the unbridgeable gap between us, unable to find a safe mooring place.

"Did he, did he say anything ..."

"Leave a note? Not unless you count a few scribbles on a notepad on his bed. Police aren't sure what to make of it. But I ... I've wondered."

"What scribbles?"

"Just two words: 'Godzilla's touch.'"

"What?"

"Godzilla. Remember what it meant to us?"

"Of course. But how would Selim know about that?"

"I used to tell him stories about our childhood friendship. I told him about Godzilla. Maybe it has something to do with ..."

"Sounds really creepy. Disturbing."

"Natalie, I still feel guilty for what happened to you." From the muffled tones, I can guess that her hand is covering the mouthpiece as she whispers into it.

"What do you mean?"

"When your father discovered us. That awful—"

"It's the past. Why bring it up now? You just lost your son."

"Because a few days before Selim died, he mentioned something to me about Cosmic Pulse."

"What did he say?" My heart starts to speed up. Fear thrums hard in my chest. Would Selim have told Faridah what he and I spoke about two years ago at Boat Quay? Maybe he needed to confess everything. Which might have included exposing me.

"I have to give you a bit of background first. When Selim was ten, I told him about that terrible incident when your father—"

"But why?"

"I wanted to coax him out from the storeroom. He had hidden himself there after Adam disciplined him. He didn't want to come out."

That word: "discipline." I hate the lie behind it.

"But why would you tell him? Of all things to tell a young boy."

I hear stifled sobbing. "I wanted him to know that he wasn't alone in feeling that terror. That it was natural, that all children fear their parents."

I cringe to hear Faridah's remark. Just how natural is it? She makes it sound unquestionable.

She continues, "He stopped crying when I told him that story about you. I crept into the storage room and sat next to my son in the semi-dark, and described your grandfather's shop. I told him about the medicine drawers with the golden embossed writing on the front. As many details as I could remember. He wiped his tears away and his mouth gawked in amazement. He forgot about his own pain. I told him what your father did to you behind

Cosmic Pulse. He asked me if you had marks like his. 'Where?' he asked. He kept insisting. He really wanted to know. So I said, 'All over her body.' He nodded, looked relieved. That was how I got him to leave his hiding place and stop crying."

A chilling shudder passes through me. I imagine a young boy of ten becoming aware of a bond between his mother's friend and him, that he and I were joined together because we had both been marked by our father's rage. I feel sick again.

"What does this have to do with ...?"

"A few days before he died, he brought up my past with you out of the blue. He insisted I ask you for forgiveness. He said, 'Don't forget Cosmic Pulse. Don't forget the love between the both of you. Remember Godzilla's touch. And save yourself.' Those were his exact words."

"So you'd told him about us."

"Yes, I told him. I wanted to." There's no hint of hesitation or regret in her voice.

"That phrase, 'Godzilla's touch.' Repeated in the note. That's why you wonder ..."

"... what it has to do with our past together. Can't be a coincidence."

"And then there's 'save yourself.'"

Silence on the line.

"Did you tell the police?"

"No," comes her whisper. "I haven't told anyone else. Not even Adam. I've thought quite a lot about what to do.

What would disclosing accomplish? It would open up a can of worms. Maybe even end up exposing too much about our past. But what for?"

"You don't think there's any purpose to that? Might offer a clue to the police."

"He's gone. That's what matters. I don't want all of us dragged through the mud. It's private; it shouldn't be disclosed to the police."

"But the police must have wondered about those words."

"Those words were meant for me." Her voice sounds resigned, yet definite. She continues, "Yes, they asked me what I thought. I said I didn't know. I said Selim liked watching old movies. And shrugged. Left it at that. Adam and Christina had nothing to say, of course." She pauses. When she speaks again, her voice is even softer, barely audible. "The police are likely to soon conclude there's been no foul play and close the case. What's past is past. I just don't get it. But maybe I need to accept that I might never know."

I feel agitated. Upset with all that I've heard so far. Surely the police would have asked standard questions. Questions like: *Did you notice any strange or unusual behaviours on his part recently? What about things he said? Any hints he was feeling despair?*

I imagine her lying to the police. She would have had to keep denying. Had to say no to those kinds of questions. Must have been difficult. There's something odd about her unwillingness to share with the police. She doesn't want to have too much exposed. But why? Perhaps the suicide feels far too exposing already.

"You know what else?" She startles me out of my musings.

"What?"

"He also said something about touch being like a pulse, and that you would know, since your grandfather took pulses the traditional way, lightly on the wrists."

This is getting too twisted for me. Am I allowed to feel angry toward the young man whom I had grown to like? His ghost still here, playing hide-and-seek with Faridah and me. His mentioning my past and what I do in my work feels as if he has implicated me in his death. I'm trying not to feel paranoid, but the sanctity of my work and my history feel threatened.

I stay quiet, trying to absorb all the details. *Don't be ridiculous*, I chide myself, *feeling threatened by a dead man*. How could I possibly know what he was talking about? *Touch like a pulse.* I'm supposed to know about touch, according to Selim, since Kong-Kong took pulses the traditional way. Puzzling. Why would he talk like that to Faridah just days before he killed himself? And repeat "Godzilla's touch" in the suicide note? He must have been hoping we would understand.

I feel guilty, even though I tell myself there's no reason to feel that way. Is it because Selim shared some of his secrets with me? Could I have saved him? Or am I supposed to figure something out? Revisit my past and somehow acquire some insight? But so what? He's gone.

I sigh, feeling the weight of things left unfinished. "I'll fly back for the memorial service."

"How long will you stay?"

"Let me see what I can do."

"That was very selfish of me, Natalie."

"Hey, I'll be there for National Day. What more could I ask for?"

I hear Adam's voice in the background.

"Sorry, must go."

The finality of that click.

AFTER the phone call, I glance up at the shelf above my desk. I scan the books on acupuncture, a handful of novels, the family photo albums and, last but not least, the tiny plastic Godzilla in the foreground. I take it off the shelf and wipe away the dust, placing it next to my laptop.

Godzilla rises from dormancy yet again. The monster that kept me company through a difficult adolescence has now acquired a new meaning, a connection to the young man who needed us to understand. But what exactly did Godzilla mean to him?

I think back to that night at Boat Quay, our long and incredibly rich conversation.

He was an unusual young man, someone who was impassioned about his connection to the past. Cared more than many people I know. We covered so much ground in that conversation. He left our meeting saying there were other things he wanted to talk to me about. If he had lived longer, he might have worked it out for himself, might have discovered ways to live more peaceably with all his contradictions.

He was obviously very proud of being related to Munshi Abdullah, the learned tutor to Raffles who, unlike popularly disseminated views, did not unequivocally support the views of his British master.

That username: Benkulen Bound. What an irony.

Benkulen was the Dutch spelling of the town at the southern tip of Sumatra. It was a busy trading post near the pepper-producing town of Silebar that came under the control of the British East India Company. In the eighteenth century, Benkulen—or Bencoolen, as the British called it—became the victim of its own success. It was the leading exporter of pepper to Europe, but its success spurred many other regions to cultivate pepper, causing the price of the commodity to fall. It was Sir Stamford Raffles, the Lieutenant-Governor of Benkulen, who subsequently suggested to the East India Company that they cede power of Benkulen to the Dutch in exchange for Malacca. Cunning chap, that Raffles. He knew that Malacca was a much more strategically useful location, in terms of trade with China.

Benkulen, on the wrong side of Sumatra, was limited by its geographic location and damned by the fallout from its own economic success. Benkulen was bound, indeed.

Shifts of power in the region during that phase of history occurred not through standard warfare but through trade negotiations, the kind of quiet surrender and conquest that played out like a game of chess. In 1824, the British did cede Benkulen to the Dutch in exchange for Malacca. Two years later, the three British settlements of Penang, Malacca and Singapore became the Straits Settlements. Later, at the close of the nineteenth century, the influx of migrants from the maritime provinces of southern China escalated and radically altered the face of Southeast Asia.

If Benkulen had not lost its status as a major trading port, then power would not have shifted to Malacca and Singapore. And if that had not happened, perhaps the fall of Malaya and Singapore to the Japanese during the Second World War would not have occurred. After all, if the Malays hadn't suffered under the racial prejudice of their colonizers, would the Malayan Communist Party have been so willing to believe the Japanese when they said they were in the region to liberate the population from the oppression of the British?

Selim was right. Everything is connected. Selim lived true to the complex, hybrid self that he was. His mind refused to simplify, refused to pretend that big notions like humanity, identity and love could be tamed with a few easy statements.

Mark my words, he had said.

Talk is only cheap if you're careless about language. But he wasn't a careless person. He was deliberate to a fault. *Believe me, Selim, I'm taking you and your words very seriously.*

After our meeting at Boat Quay, we kept in touch through email and frequent text messaging. He had lots of chances to tell me. So why didn't he say anything about the impact of my childhood experiences on him? Why would he wait more than two years before he told his mother to ask me for forgiveness? Days before he died.

Investigate history, he had said. His suicide forces me to ask troubling questions. I must do my best to discover what I can.

"What's the point of talking about the past?" Mum often says to me. Maybe that's why she hardly talks about Kong-Kong and Mah-Mah these days. A prohibitive silence, like a dark, outstretched shadow, has been enforced over the years, preventing us from seeing clearly.

Remember Godzilla's touch. Touch like a pulse.

I'm supposed to know? My miniature Godzilla sits on the desk, waiting.

There's a belief in Shinto Buddhism that inanimate figures acquire life from the energy we invest in them. Worshippers carve wooden figures of gods and goddesses and thereby imbue them with life through their devotion.

In contrast, consumers nowadays are fascinated by *figua*, the plastic toy characters derived from manga novels and video games. Unlike the Shinto carvers, we haven't created the *figua* ourselves.

But still. How easily we humans become possessed by our possessions.

four 脈

"Granddaughter, you look this row of shop houses," Kong-Kong said in a halting Mandarin inflected with a Shanghainese accent, waving his arms in the air as we stood in front of Cosmic Pulse. "Only Chinese people enough smart do business. Make money, everything proper place. You see Malays, only know how to fish and sit around *kampong.*" My grandfather was fond of sweeping statements, especially if he was the one who made them. After the confident proclamation in his asthmatic, raspy voice, he made that too-familiar movement with his mouth and spat a huge yellow gob onto the pavement, then recited:

Tzi zong tzi du
Vok tieo mo mi chu
Vong zong tiau du
Vok tieo chu zhu du

The Hakka proverb cautioned thus: If you have straight innards, your cooking pot will be empty of rice, but if you can be a little crooked, your pot will be filled with the best food.

I gazed up at Kong-Kong's tall stature, his face darkened by the scorching noonday sun behind him. I blinked at his formidable presence, then past him to the upper windows above the shop. They were like large eyes, shuttered and painted a dark green, in contrast to the pale yellow walls of the façade.

It puzzled me how Kong-Kong came to discover truths about Malays and could proclaim them with such certainty. Laced with vehemence. I was not quite six and often puzzled by the kinds of pronouncements adults would make. Where did they go to learn these things, and why didn't I know?

My family never talked about our Malay lineage. On Mum's side, Mah-Mah was Nonya, the female offspring of a Chinese father and a Malay mother. But Kong-Kong never commented on it, as if this uncomfortable reality didn't exist. He talked to us as if Malayness was foreign to us.

My parents and I lived above Kong-Kong's herbal shop from 1965 until we left Singapore for Toronto. I still think of those quiet, dark rooms as "the house." For the first five and a half years of my life, my parents and I had lived at my grandparents' house on Koon Seng Road. At the big house, I saw Kong-Kong and Mah-Mah and Uncle late in the evenings after they returned from work. After Papa, Mum and I moved to the rooms above the shop, I saw my grandparents and uncle for most of the day, but hardly ever in the evenings.

Cosmic Pulse was the only Chinese herbal medicine business in a row of narrow shop houses clustered together on Joo Chiat Road. Hence, my Kong-Kong, Tian Hee, was well known in the area and sought for his skill as a herbalist.

Joo Chiat Road was a major thoroughfare in Katong that ran approximately north-south, dividing Koon Seng Road from its western twin, Dunman Road. Pulse—as I called it—stood out in the swiftly developing Katong area, with its large rosewood sign above the wide front entrance. The unusual name was beautifully carved and emblazoned in gold.

Kong-Kong was proud that his family lived in Katong, because it gave him affinity with wealthy Chinese merchants, especially Chew Joo Chiat, for whom the road was named.

The corridor in front of those shop houses on either side of Cosmic Pulse became my playground, where I could race from one end to the other. On the southern edge of the row of shops was a dentist, while at the north corner stood a smallish *kopi tiam* coffee shop dominated by the roti paratha seller.

I spent a substantial amount of time as a preschooler observing the Indian hawker whose daily garb was a tattered, oil-stained T-shirt paired with a purple and white chequered sarong. I loved watching Paratha Man, how fast his nimble fingers worked, the flair with which he could fling and stretch a round of dough into a thin disc in mid-air before laying each circle of dough onto the iron griddle, heated by a wood-fed fire. His moist, puffy rotis, well greased with copious amounts of ghee, were extremely popular. In the early mornings, a steady flow of office workers and labourers alike began their day with an order of paratha and accompanying curry, washed down with *kopi-O*, coffee drunk black, or *kopi-C*, sweetened with condensed milk.

There were many mornings when I sat in the *kopi tiam* with Mum before she started her day at Cosmic Pulse. Too young to drink coffee, I sat with my glass of hot barley drink while my mother drank her coffee black. I liked staring into her eyes, defined by her fashionable cat's eye glasses, and wondered if the local brew was somehow responsible for the deep, rich black of her eyes. I often played with my "five stones"—the cloth pyramids my mother had sewn for me, stuffed with raw mung beans. Meanwhile, Mum would read one of her Qiong Yao novels, stealing precious time before returning to Kong-Kong's shop.

At the southern end of our row, the dentist's office gave off the overpowering smell of Dettol and a mix of terrifyingly pungent anaesthetics. Next to the dentist was a narrow alley down which motorcycles, scooters, bicycles and three-wheeled carts would travel willy-nilly, without any regard for pedestrians. It was drummed into me early on never to attempt to cross such dangerous straits unaccompanied.

Cosmic Pulse, as I grew to understand later, was an extremely odd name for a herbal medicine shop. As Mum said, *Your Kong-Kong, he a bit crazy, one hand place on abacus, other one point to Heaven.*

My grandfather Tian was proud of his origins, as well as his eccentric indulgences. *Men*, he used to say, *need wander far away from home*. His father was a cobbler who, as a young man, left the village for Shanghai and worked his way up until he eventually became the owner of a reputable shoe store frequented by wealthy Chinese, as well as European and Japanese travellers. His only son wasn't interested in merely inheriting his father's wealth; he had dreams of travelling across the ocean. He knew of Singapore, of many merchants and labourers who made their way there. Tian wanted to try something entirely different. He would learn to be a herbalist instead. There was something very appealing about repairing unseen malaise. Kong-Kong had been an idealist and a daydreamer from early on—even taking part in the student protests against the Manchurian Incident in 1931. A few months after the

Japanese navy bombed Shanghai on January 28, 1932, his family realized that it might be wise to support their son's aspirations to leave the city.

Soon after he reached Singapore at age twenty, Tian adopted an English name, calling himself Conrad after Joseph Conrad, the famous British writer. He felt they shared some things in common, such as a love of seafaring. It was the lure of exotic adventure that gave life meaning, he said, quoting Conrad: *"Faith is a myth and beliefs shift like mists on the shore."*

He would first recite the quote in Mandarin, then in English. He had read Conrad in translation, but he was such a fan that he sought out the original version so he could memorize the quotes he liked in the King's English. Kong-Kong seldom used English, but when he quoted Conrad it was impeccable. When he used the language colloquially, he often left out the singular and plural indicators, past, present and future tenses, and sometimes prepositions. Everyone was a *he* in Kong-Kong's speech, and English was not going to make him change that.

His parents had connections to the overseas Chinese communities in Southeast Asia, and arranged for him to marry a young woman, not quite fifteen, the daughter of a rubber plantation tycoon in Malacca. They felt it was important to marry their son off before he had a chance to fall prey to the wiles of the new country, there being ample opportunities for lonely men to succumb to illicit carnal diversions in Singapore.

My grandmother was that young girl. Mah-Mah described her young self as a sulky introvert who liked daydreaming to the "Blue Danube" crackling from the gramophone. Siew Lian had a tutor who, besides teaching her English and Mandarin, also showed her how to use a divination method popular in China. In the evenings, bored with sitting around the house, she insisted on going out to the fields in search of fireflies and the music of cicadas.

Siew Lian met her groom a month before their marriage. *He came in trishaw*, she would say to me, smiling at the memory of the awkward suitor arriving at her father's Malaccan mansion on Jalan Tun Tan Cheng Lock, dressed in a Western suit, with wrinkled trousers that barely reached the ankles. She forgave his shabby suit, impressed by the decisive parting of greasily pomaded hair on the left side of his head and the sly, mischievous way he glanced up at her.

"You know why store have this name? Name for me," Mah-Mah told me.

"Not true, granddaughter," Kong-Kong retorted in Mandarin. "This name Cosmic Pulse because as young man, I follow my adventurous spirit. Look to heaven because stars in sky pulse for those who want to see." Once again, he reverted to Conrad in impeccable English: "*It was the stillness of an implacable force brooding over an inscrutable intention.*"

It didn't take long for Tian to set up Cosmic Pulse. When he first arrived in Singapore, he worked in someone else's shop for a few years. He started his own business when my mother was a toddler. His young wife, already pregnant with their second child, did not like being bored, so she began using her divination skills for clients in the back room.

These were the stories I was regaled with as I grew up. In my own early memories of the store, Kong-Kong was already in his fifties, and Mah-Mah worked at the counter, assisting her husband with the dispensing of medicines, while Uncle, Mama's younger brother, made deliveries on his bicycle or else loitered in the back, smoking stinky hand-rolled cigarettes.

IN THE '60s, Singapore was caught in the swirl of tremendous transitions. In September 1963, Singapore, along with Sabah and Sarawak, joined the Federation of Malaya to form Malaysia. The ideological differences between the Singaporean and Malayan governments, however, were far too great, resulting in disagreements over politics and financial and social policies. The conflict spread to the populace and exploded in the race riots in 1964. The next year, the Malaysian government, under Tunku Abdul Rahman, dropped Singapore from the federation, causing the prime minister, Lee Kuan Yew, to weep on national TV.

Western ways were becoming more popular, especially the increasing use of English in the public sphere. There was a bit of Mandarin used then, but far less than you hear nowadays in Singapore. Instead, my ears were attuned to the sounds of many Chinese dialects—Hokkien, Teochew and Cantonese, for example—as well as Malay and Tamil. Music blared from clunky jukeboxes in coffee shops and restaurants: strains of Elvis Presley singing "Love Me Tender," or Connie Francis pining for "Young Love," alongside Mandarin love songs sung by Chow Hsuan and Bai Kwong and the occasional Malay ballad.

The walls of Cosmic Pulse were covered floor to ceiling with dark-stained elm apothecary drawers filled with herbs, each drawer marked clearly with gold Chinese script. Pulse's atmosphere varied: sometimes it was sombre to a fault, but there were occasions when the shop was dominated by loud chatter. It depended mostly on Kong-Kong's mood. If he was having a cheerful day, everyone else, down to the only paid shop assistant who was not family, would laugh and move about as if all under heaven was flowing in harmony. If Kong-Kong suffered one of his black moods, however, Cosmic Pulse registered his distress in its own troubled rhythms, skipping and wavering like the pulse of a sick person.

Regardless of the atmosphere, Kong-Kong's business thrived because of his talent at concocting brews to heal the afflicted. Over the years, I would learn to recognize the different herbs and animal parts, and become familiar with their uses.

The other activity at the shop revolved around Mah-Mah's gift of divination. At the back of the shop, past the ladders leaning against the walls of apothecary drawers, was a small room separated from the corridor by indigo blue cotton curtains. In this sanctuary, Mah-Mah practised her art, conducting sessions for those who sought her unique kind of help. The querent would throw onto the table twelve wooden chips emblazoned with Chinese symbols—four for Heaven, four for Earth and four for Humanity. Mah-Mah would consult the book known to me as the Oracle, decoding the trigraphs that appeared with each throw.

During her sessions, I would either sit on her lap or next to her, on top of a stool stacked with dusty volumes of Chinese *materia medica*. I was enraptured. I puzzled over Mah-Mah's kind of religion. It was so unlike my father's Christianity. Instead of the Holy Trinity of Father, Son and Holy Spirit, her language consisted of Heaven, Man and Earth, with each force influencing the others. I later recognized this language as Taoist. Mah-Mah's divination sessions opened me up to a world very different than Sunday church service with my parents.

Mah-Mah's and Kong-Kong's influence led me to grow up believing that there existed a cosmic pulse throughout the universe, and that it behooved us lowly humans to seek advice and direction from the myriad forces around us.

Mum didn't mind at all that I was learning divination. Accustomed to her mother's ways, she simply regarded it as another pastime to entertain me. Besides, it freed her up to do household chores. She was prudent enough to warn me against telling Papa, who considered Mah-Mah's skill to be the sinister work of the devil.

At the back of Cosmic Pulse was the kitchen area, with three firewood stoves set into concrete blocks. Pyramids of firewood and charcoal in buckets were left close to the stoves, along with a large bamboo fan for raising the flames.

The kitchen opened out through wooden, latticed doors into a courtyard. Sitting in the courtyard, I could look up at the sky overhead; I thought of that rectangular opening as the sky window. Sunlight filtered down at an angle, allowing a softer, diffuse light. Right below the sky window was a well of sorts, broader than it was deep, a receptacle for water from the tap.

A flurry of laundry hung on the lines, mostly long, thin strips of cotton, stained and yellowed from poultices that Kong-Kong wrapped around his patients' bodies. A couple of stools stood next to the well.

At the far end of the courtyard was the perennially stinky bucket latrine. A flight of creaky stairs next to it led to our rooms above.

My parents and I lived a shadowy existence, eclipsed by the noisy public face of Cosmic Pulse below us. Our living room doubled as dining room, while the two smaller rooms were our bedrooms. Mum cooked downstairs, using a small, freestanding charcoal stove in the courtyard. All the rooms had wooden latticed windows that opened onto the courtyard below. One of my favourite spots was in the living room, where there was a peephole in the wooden floor. I liked to remove the circular piece of wood and look down onto the pavement below, just outside the shop entrance, so I could see who was coming and going from Pulse.

In the daytime, Hwi the shop assistant was often in the kitchen, monitoring several clay pots of herbs being brewed on the large stoves while he fanned the flames vigorously with the bamboo fan. There would often be at least two, if not three, pots on the go at once. Sweat dribbled down his forehead, on either side of his prominent northern Chinese nose and down his gaunt cheekbones, but he rarely bothered to wipe his face. He would be in trouble with Kong-Kong if his attention lapsed. Hwi possessed a wiry, taut torso. He darted about as if stricken with a perpetual bout of nerves. Occasionally, he snorted loudly, and I learned this meant he was annoyed at being run off his feet by errands. Snorting was Hwi's way of expressing irritation at my grandfather's unreasonable expectations. I would watch him from my perch on a stool beside the well, dipping my fingers into the water and splashing it on my skin to cool off. These were my favourite moments, when I was the secret watcher, spared the scrutiny of others.

If I happened to be in the shop, caught up in the bustle, I liked to sit at the display counter. I enjoyed observing Kong-Kong's bony hands, steady and decisive, as he tipped herbs out from the copper pan of the *daching* measuring instrument onto large pieces of manila paper. Some of my most vivid memories of Cosmic Pulse are associated with sounds: the clink of the copper pan and the soft clicking of abacus beads struck against one another as he worked out the cost of the medicines.

"Concentrate here, in front," he would often say, tapping me between the collar bones, just above my heart, "not worry past or future. Live this moment, you understand?"

"Is that how you got to be so good at measuring herbs?"

"Tell your father stop foolish, come work for me." He gave me one of his I-know-best nods. I knew that Kong-Kong disapproved of Papa working as a salesman for the pharmaceutical company.

Why did all of Kong-Kong's brews have to smell so foul? The steamy stench curled up from the spouts of those clay pots as Hwi squatted in front of the stove, watching like a hawk. I would pinch my nose and open my mouth wide to breathe. Papa's pills, on the other hand, despite residing in his smelly leather bag, were quite free of any odour. They smelled of nothing. They were just different shapes and colours, and if you closed your eyes, it was rather hard to tell which ones were which.

Next to Cosmic Pulse was a provision shop that sold basic goods such as bags of rice, dried beans and salted fish. The shop was also stocked with various kinds of candy and daily necessities like tools, mosquito coils, Darkie toothpaste, Listerine and Bayer's Aspirin.

The Lim family, who ran the provision shop, owned a black-and-white TV that they only switched on in the evenings. At that time of night, almost all the wooden slats were placed into their slots at the entrance, leaving a gap wide enough for one adult body to squeeze through. Inside, in the darkness, the Lims would gather together in front of the one spot of luminous brightness, their precious Rediffusion TV screen, watching Chinese soaps. The six of them, parents and four children, would huddle close. Something about that closeness disquieted me. We didn't have a television at the time. I often longed to join the Lims and pretend I was part of that family. The eerie yet magical light from the Lims' TV would taunt me until my parents acquired a television set years later.

In place of TV, I entertained myself by studying the movement of light dancing on the water in the large, rectangular well. I told myself this was better than any television show. I knew intimately all the moods of slanted light, how it formed reflections on the water directly under the sky window. Clouds drifted overhead, dancing guests from ancient China or, sometimes, characters from my Sunday school picture books. Prophets such as Elijah and Jeremiah made frequent appearances, with their trailing beards and big eyes.

It was a particularly humid day, on the eve of the Chinese New Year in 1965, when I had my first experience of the invisible realms. As was my habit, I was staring into the well, frequently splashing water on my face while watching the clouds' changing reflections. Storm clouds were gathering overhead. A strong wind stirred the heavy air, causing tiny ripples to disrupt the placid surface of the water.

I was humming quietly. *Jesus loves me, this I know, for the Bible tells me so, little ones to Him belong* . . .

It only takes a moment for one's world to be altered irrevocably. The water disappeared, and in its place a light appeared, so strong it hurt my eyes. I blinked once, twice, and soon adjusted to the piercing brightness. Shapes began to form inside that light, shapes that did not reflect the landscape of the sky overhead. I could make out tall beings standing among white horses. The beings resembled humans, except they had slender, muscular wings along the length of their torsos. The vibrations from their wings reached me, penetrating me like pulses of light.

"Natalie, don't put your hands into the water! So dirty!"

I bolted upright to stare into Mum's eyes, framed by those beautiful glasses. She stepped into the courtyard from the kitchen and pulled my hands out of the water.

"How many times I say, no playing with water!"

I stared into the well. The creatures were gone. The well was full of ordinary water, reflecting the sky.

"Dream," I muttered, for there were no words to describe what I had seen. And certainly no words for the disappointment I felt at the loss of magic. My fingers felt itchy again. I looked at them. Just under the skin were the tiniest eyes filled with liquid. I peeled off some skin, bursting the eyes and exposing the rawness underneath.

"Natalie! Come here," called Mah-Mah, beckoning from inside her room.

Mah-Mah was waving her elegant sandalwood fan rhythmically in front of her face. The first two press studs on her greyish blue samfu were undone, exposing her neck and right shoulder and the white cotton tunic underneath. The wooden chips of her trade were spread out randomly on the table. Next to the chips was a tall glass of Ribena, the ice cubes snapping as they cracked and melted. Mah-Mah moved the volumes of *materia medica* from the stool onto the rattan chair and gestured for me to sit there, facing her. This was the seat usually reserved for her paying customers. I dangled my legs loosely, swinging them under the table and occasionally hitting my foot against the crossbeam of the table. "One-two, one-two-three, one-two, one-two-three," I muttered, as I swung my legs back and forth.

"Want haw flakes?" Mah-Mah tore open the thumb-sized cylindrical packet and handed me a few of the thin red rounds. I popped two into my mouth and tasted the sweet, soft tanginess as they melted slowly on my tongue.

"Is it true, this store is named for you?" I asked once again.

"Of course. I told you, many times already."

"Kong-Kong said it's named for some white man."

Mah-Mah's mouth turned down into an unpleasant snarl. "Don't pay him attention. Listen." She tapped me gently on my wrist, right where I had often seen Kong-Kong place his fingers to take a patient's pulse. "Special gift I have. You my first grandchild, I think you also have. Pay attention to Oracle. When you older, I teach you tri-graphs, one by one." She peered into my eyes, as if she was searching for an answer to a question. "Eyes cannot lie."

I shuddered, feeling the force of Mah-Mah's attention on me, and then I shook my head vigorously, trying to shake images of those strange creatures out of my head.

"You saying no?"

"I don't know what you mean, Mah-Mah."

She smiled warmly at me. "Never mind. The time will come when you will know."

I felt a shiver run through me, as if my body under-stood the truth of Mah-Mah's wisdom long before my mind did.

Maybe that was why I felt rather subdued later that night as Kong-Kong, Mah-Mah, Uncle, Mum and I ate our hot-pot dinner in the big house on Koon Seng Road.

The house was set about fifty feet back from Koon Seng Road. The largest house on that stretch of road, it was a combination of European architectural influences and local imagination.

Even though it was Chinese New Year's Eve, Papa was still not home. I had no idea why, but I could see the glances my grandparents were throwing in my mother's direction. Accusatory, as if she had done something wrong.

In contrast to the heat of the day, my grandparents' house sent a deep chill through me, despite the cause for celebration. Loud clanging of percussion instruments and shrill voices filtered through to us from the Taoist temple nearby on Everitt Road; I could hear a Cantonese opera being performed on the makeshift stage in front of the temple.

The main floor of my grandparents' house was dark except for two overhead lamps that illuminated the long rosewood dining table. A naked bulb lit up the servants' eating area in the kitchen behind, just visible through the vertical iron bars of the large floor-to-ceiling windows. I could make out the half-lit silhouettes of my grandparents' cook and amah eating dinner at their table. They ate quietly but briskly, shoving food into their mouths.

The faraway sounds of the opera enticed me. "Please, can we go watch?" I placed my hand on Mum's thigh and shook it, pleadingly.

Mum looked at me without answering.

"*Gang bei*, drink up!" Kong-Kong's voice boomed.

"Yeah, Ah Pak, don't wait for me, huh!" Uncle teased his father.

Kong-Kong and Uncle were egging one another on with their toasts, downing their tiny cups of hot, fragrant Chinese wine. Chopsticks rapped against each other and against the Ming blue porcelain bowls as my family supped heartily. Mum put cooked fish balls and vegetables in my bowl, breaking up the fish balls so they weren't too hot for me. I stared into the unlit front reception hall, remembering those strange creatures I had seen earlier in the day, at the back of Cosmic Pulse.

"Where is Papa?" I gazed up with puzzlement at my mother.

"Eat," she replied, seeming not to have heard my question.

"Eh, granddaughter, why you frown like old woman with no future?" Kong-Kong rapped his knuckles on my head.

I straightened up from my slouch. I hated it when Kong-Kong knocked on my head like that, but at least he wasn't using a rolled-up newspaper to whack me this time.

"Ah Pak, she always daydream. Don't mind her," replied Mum.

Mah-Mah leaned down toward me. "Daydreams only talented few allowed. Not everybody can do," she whispered encouragingly.

I watched the adults eating and talking at the table. There were things that couldn't be told to adults, and my afternoon experience was one of them. I was sure of it. Adults had their own ideas about what was right or wrong, and I had a feeling they would think what had happened to me was very wrong indeed. Except perhaps for Mah-Mah.

"Why my son-in-law busybody other people's business, ignore family, even on New Year Eve, huh?" Mah-Mah clucked in a disapproving tone.

"Heng said he home in time. No idea what happened," came Mum's uncertain reply.

A short while later, we heard Papa's voice from the front garden, letting out a shout. Sounds of scuffling and loud thuds filtered in.

Mah-Mah didn't show any expression on her face. It was impossible to guess what she was feeling. But I knew my own fear, a feeling that weighted me to my seat, preventing me from moving.

My mother got up from the table and rushed out. "Heng!"

Kong-Kong started to cough and wheeze. My eyes turned toward the back of the house when Ah See noisily pushed aside her bamboo chair in the kitchen. She moved briskly past us, entering the unlit reception hall for mere seconds before she reappeared with some pills for Kong-Kong.

My heart was pounding very fast. Uncle reached out to grip my chin tightly between his fingers. "Scared? Girl, you hopeless!"

I stood up. My legs were wobbly and weak, but I forced myself to walk slowly through the dark hall toward the front entrance. Through the door, I saw Papa in the garden, dimly lit by the street lamp. He was crouched low to the ground, hand holding his jaw. His lip was cut, and there was blood splattered all over his white shirt.

I shivered, the hairs on my neck standing on end. My whole body started to shake uncontrollably. My arms were at my sides. I stretched my fingers down, reaching for the earth.

Mum stared sternly at me. "Go inside."

My feet wouldn't budge. There was some powerful force keeping me rooted there, staring at that scene in the front garden. It was Chinese New Year the next day, a New Moon, the beginning of the Year of the Wood Snake. But instead of a healthy snake, there Papa was in the front garden, bruised and bleeding. It felt wrong.

Mum helped Papa into the house. But I didn't follow them back in. Instead, I stood there in the doorway and looked at my wooden horse on the front porch as I listened to the muffled voices of the adults inside.

"Girl, come in!" came my father's command.

I forced myself to face the dark interior of the house and, with slow steps, approached my family gathered around the dining table.

He was sitting on one of the dining chairs. Mum was dabbing the cut on his cheek with a wad of cotton soaked in gentian violet. He winced from the pain.

Mah-Mah looked sternly at her son-in-law. "Best stay out of other people business."

"I was trying to help. Otherwise, who knows what that man would have done to her?"

"I wonder your story," retorted my grandmother, not even bothering to hide her skepticism.

Papa turned away from her and looked at me hiding in the dark corner. "Come out of the shadow! Show me your hands! Still peeling them?"

I walked cautiously toward Papa, but when I was close enough, he yanked me closer by pulling at my sleeve. I started to tremble again, this time from fear of my father's disfigured face, his lips bloodied and swollen, a line of blood streaming down from his forehead while a burst of crimson covered his nose.

"You need lesson?" He grabbed the scissors on the table. In a cool voice he said, "You don't stop peeling, I cut all your fingers off. Like this, okay?" Then he snipped at the noodles in the serving dish.

Kong-Kong frowned disapprovingly at my father, but Uncle laughed out loud and continued to drink wine.

"Stop it," Mah-Mah's voice rang out. "No fighting on New Year Eve. Very bad luck."

I pulled away from Papa and ran to the front entrance. I looked up at the sky. I could smell the warning in the air, a damp intensity that seeped into my skin. A torrential rain was coming. I wondered why the world was so full of upsetting things. I wished the ache that was growing inside would leave me, but try as I might, nothing I did seemed to make that pain go away. Instead, the ache reached deep down into my feet and wrapped itself around both my heels, refusing to leave.

I stared into the distance. Lights from the opera stage outside the temple sparkled. I forced myself to pay attention to the melodies being sung, unfamiliar and lilting, nothing like the hymns I was used to in church.

After an eternity, Ah See came up to me, placed a hand lightly on my shoulder and said, "Your mother say we can watch opera. Come, I take you."

We slipped our feet into red clogs. They kept time with the soft clash of cymbals in the background as we hurried toward the string of bright lights, Ah See holding firmly onto my hand.

The smell of incense tickled my nostrils. I inhaled deeply, enjoying the rich aromas. People were standing about, mothers with babies slung on their backs, men marked by red-tipped cigarettes hanging from their mouths, children scurrying about. A few folks were right at the front, seated on stools they had brought. Ah See and I made our way closer to the stage.

My hands started to itch again. I pulled away from Ah See's grip so I could scratch my fingers. She took my hand gently in hers again and said, "When we home, I put ointment on itchy hands, okay?"

The opera singers were moving briskly about, as if in a chase. The heroine stroked the pair of lovely, feathery protuberances that sprouted from either side of her costume. Curvaceous and pliable, were they meant to be wings? The heroine looked like a butterfly let loose in the bright heaven.

Ah See bent down to whisper into my ear, "You see how warrior woman ride horse and she escape bad men?"

I glanced at her. She had straightened up and was directing her attention completely at the stage. Her eyes did not stray from the unfolding drama as her hand now rested firmly on my shoulder.

five 脈

Just past noon on Sunday. People spill from inside the church onto the pavement outside on Sullivan, the children, as usual, talented at darting around and squeezing past adults. Most of these children will leave home once they reach eighteen or nineteen. At the latest, in their twenties. It's different in Asia. Plenty of people live at home long into their adulthood. And some, like me, take care of their parents.

In the scorching sunlight, I have to shield my eyes with one hand as I hold onto Papa, guiding him out of the way of the emerging crowd. He balances on his other side with a cane, albeit shakily. Meanwhile, Mum lingers in the dim, cool shadow of the foyer, talking to the pastor.

I think of that night in 1965 when Papa arrived late for Chinese New Year's Eve at my grandparents' house. How terrified I was when Papa threatened to cut off my fingers if I didn't stop peeling. My body shook for a long time after.

Forty years later, when I turned around that winter evening in 2005 to see Papa's body prone on the snowy sidewalk in front of our house on Baldwin, I began to shake like that. But for a different reason. Life had taken a drastic turn. The man I had been so terrified of was gone. With that realization, I became a changed person.

How frail Papa looks now. His body has wilted ever since the stroke.

I look across Beverley Street to the fenced perimeter of the park. Grange Park is one of my favourite places. I go there whenever I need to pretend that there's no one else I'm responsible for. I sit on a bench for an hour or so, listening to the sound of the wind stirring the delicate leaves of the trees overhead.

I stare at the park wistfully, admiring the dappled shade afforded by the trees in the midday sun. Wish I could be there now, by myself. Free of obligations. I think of my taiji mornings there. White Crane Flashes Its Wings, Single Whip, Wave Hands like Clouds. I'm imagining my body moving softly through the air, all the while holding onto Papa's shoulder and doing the minimal exchange of greetings.

Around us, people are chatting in Cantonese. Many of them left Hong Kong in the late '80s or '90s, long before the handover of Hong Kong to the mainland in July 1997. Thanks to coming to this church, I've improved my Cantonese. I might even pass as a Hong Konger. It doesn't matter to me that I don't have the same kind of faith as many others at this church. There's virtue in keeping certain secrets. What matters is that my parents have found a community of people to share life with.

Mr. Chan drives Papa and Mum the short distance down to Swatow restaurant, but I choose to walk, lagging behind the talkers. In the swirl of the Sunday crowd along Spadina, my mind turns inward, tracing the changes in me since Papa's collapse.

All the rules I had lived by, all the cherished prohibitions crumbled away and no longer had the capacity to sustain my denial. Rage surged through me. Tortured by a litany of his past wrongs, I felt the urge to strike or pull him as I helped him move, eat or lie down.

I'm glad I didn't stay locked in that state of mind. I made myself act kindly despite my anger. Sometimes magic isn't dramatic. Rage was a ghost that—upon discovering its diminished relevance to present circumstances—had to resign itself to eventually departing.

I'll never know the true reason for Papa's unhappiness. But I know I don't want to become like him, don't want to hold someone else responsible for my happiness.

I bring myself back to the present. The intersection of Dundas and Spadina in Chinatown has got to be one of the most chaotic and colourful scenes in Canada. I love the bustle and squeeze, the frenetic shouts of street vendors intent on selling you cheap socks and underwear. Cheap everything.

Today, there's a guy from mainland China trying to sell off his grandfather's military mementos from the 1949 Long March and various campaigns of the Communist government. He even has a Japanese soldier's badge, a copper-embossed image of a sage-like profile. There are many browsers, but only a few handle the memorabilia. Maybe it's because they feel uneasy touching remnants of a violent era. Especially if their families were affected.

A few feet north of the vendor is a lanky blind man with a flowing mane of white hair. He plays "Yellow Submarine" on his bamboo flute, his white cane tucked under one armpit. His baseball cap on the ground is graced with a few loonies and quarters.

Lunch goes by quickly. By the time the Chans drop us off in front of the house, it's almost two o'clock. Mum rushes ahead of us to unlock the door, while I assist Papa safely out of the car. Our house is the only yellow one in the middle of a block of red-bricked townhouses. The front yard is rather plain, a patch of grass with a single, but impressive, maple. There are two low front steps from the walkway to the porch, fairly manageable for Papa, whose slow shuffle takes about three minutes from the front door to his Ikea recliner in the living room. In the kitchen, out of Papa's earshot, I begin my disclosure the moment Mum sits down with her cup of freshly brewed

Malaccan coffee, sweetened with loads of sugar and drunk black.

"I have to go back to Singapore on Wednesday."

"What?" She blinks at me, sipping loudly.

"Something tragic has happened."

She stares blankly at me, waiting.

"A friend's son has died suddenly."

"Who?"

"Selim. Gabriel Khoo."

"Who?"

"Faridah's son."

Mum takes another long sip of coffee before she reaches out to grab a handful of red melon seeds from the bowl on the table.

"Faridah? You still in touch with her?" Her left eyebrow rises in a show of surprise, although I don't feel any hint of disapproval.

I nod. "Got the letter four days ago."

"So young. What happened?"

"Died suddenly," I reply, hoping she won't ask for more details.

"Very sad. World full of sad things."

She cracks open one melon seed after another, piling the carcasses neatly in a small mound in front of her. Melon seeds are a vastly underrated coping strategy for what ails us. If only more people would sit quietly eating melon seeds while in the midst of distress, there might be less grief in the world.

"You'll be okay, huh? Get rides to physiotherapy from Mrs. Wong at church and call Judy for extra help?"

Without looking up from her pile of melon seed husks, she answers, "Yeah, sure."

I yawn. Doesn't look right, but this happens whenever I feel overcome by the tension of what's not being discussed. I stare at the bags of groceries from our shopping trip in Chinatown. Huddled next to the refrigerator. Even the sight of them feels a bit overwhelming at this moment. *Put us away quickly, before it's too late*, I imagine them screaming at us. After a suitably long pause, I say, "I'll go check on Papa."

In the living room, Papa's eyes flicker ever so slightly when I enter. I grab a tissue to wipe off some drool that has formed on the right side of his mouth.

Instead of rage, I feel a lot of sadness these days. And pity. My father has become impossible and inaccessible in an entirely different way.

"What about *Shaolin Soccer*, Papa?" I ask, as I wave the DVD in front of him.

He blinks twice.

I leave him to the movie and retreat upstairs to my room. Quickly put on my headphones and tune in to CBC. The composer Christos Hatzis is being interviewed. In a gentle tone, he says that he creates music to counter the fragmentation in the world. A long composition with voices and orchestra comes on, winding through my consciousness. Soothing and powerful at the same time.

When the music ends, I pick up my cellphone and click open the inbox, scrolling down to Selim's text messages, which he started sending soon after we met at Boat Quay.

upset @ me for jnng police. wht's sh so tnse abt?
mom frgttn wht it's lke to be yng & advntrous?
BB

Benkulen Bound said a lot with very little. His text messaging persona was, however, slightly different than the Selim I had that long conversation with. The sardonic tone of his texts would leave me wondering about the fragility he tried to hide. As I reread his subsequent messages, I picture him sitting at Harry's Bar, turning away when he didn't want to be completely direct. But I sensed his vulnerability, regardless.

If a text message seems disembodied, it's only because the receiver knows little or nothing of the sender's facial expressions, the nuance revealed in the way someone uses his body. The body communicates so eloquently. And I enjoy paying attention to that language.

So I would always hearken back to my direct experience of being with him to help me interpret his messages. Selim's text messaging was ruled by the language of innuendo; he relied heavily on the art of the question, even feigning haughty disdain at times. I could relate to that kind of camouflage. He was so good at being cautious. If I hadn't met him for drinks that evening, I would have read his text messages entirely wrongly and taken him to be a cold cynic. But he was actually the opposite of that.

Where was the coincidence in the fact that we shared many things in common? Rage toward our fathers. Our love for Faridah. Immersion in the practice of Kinbaku. The feel of the rope in the hands, against the skin. Except that we occupied different roles in the practice. Like most practitioners of the rope, we lived underground lives seemingly at odds with our outer personae.

impssbl 2 expln 2 sme 1 who dsnt hve same need. crave a gr8er rush. nvr feels exctng enuf. want > edge. lookng 4 thse wh cn master fear, go bynd.
BB

It's not fair to generalize. Kink, like any human invention, is a matter of definition. Although Selim and I met in the Kinbaku chat room, we came to the practice with very different needs. I never got around to attempting to answer the question about good pain versus bad pain that he had posed to me that night at Harry's Bar.

What had created his need to experience pain? Was it because he had been beaten by his father? I was beaten by Papa, but I don't want to experience that kind of pain, not to any degree, however mild. Nor do I wish to inflict pain. But Selim was unwavering in his dedication to feeling pain, fulfilling that need as the slave in a Kinbaku scene.

Oddly enough, I came to Kinbaku through my acupuncture practice. A man came for his first session about three years ago and asked if I could do some special work with him. He said his request was unusual and then proceeded to strip down to display a stunning pattern of marks across his torso. "Can you put needles at the points where the marks intersect?"

It turned out he had been reading websites about acupuncture meridians. He was convinced there was a way to do Japanese bondage to maximize the healing potential of the rope patterns, working the points of intersection as ways to tonify and regulate the blood or to disperse energy blockages. He had tried to seek the help of other acupuncturists for this venture, but the three he had asked before me had all turned him down. "Obviously they think I'm a freak," he said.

This last comment sounded appealing. After all, I had never felt particularly normal myself. I admired the patterns made by the rope on his body. I pressed on his skin in a few places. I was impressed that the points of intersection of the rope often coincided with various acupuncture points. Besides, he had a beautiful body. Not just physically, but because he possessed an energy that radiated excitement, a certain raw enthusiasm. I liked his dedication to an unusual cause. Liked that he needed some special attention that only someone with my training could provide. It didn't take me long to reply that I would be willing to help him, but only if he taught me Kinbaku.

mom shld've foll hr heart instd of tradtn. it's abt gng
past fear. cant wait around. or luv tht's unrequited will
kill u.
BB

Selim liked codes, making and breaking them. Reread-
ing his text messages, I notice the words he chose to spell
out completely, as if he couldn't bear to shorten them.
Why? Was it mere coincidence? For instance, the word
"heart."

Then there was the one-liner.

i hate being bored.

Which echoed the kinds of things he had said to me
that evening at Harry's, as we drank Tiger beer. How had
he put it? Feeling discomforted by comforting notions?
Wait, I have it reversed. He said that he didn't want to take
comfort in discomforting notions.

I open the last text message, sent only weeks before he
died.

yr chldhd stories saved me. tell u in prsn. cant wait.

Why did Selim mention Godzilla to his mother?
There's so much I will never know.

six 脈

When I first met Faridah Mohammed in our Secondary One class, I was intrigued by the fairness of her skin. Shouldn't she be dark, given her last name?

The year was 1972, and we were thirteen.

"Your skin so pale! Like mangosteen flesh."

"Huh? Your tongue so blunt? Gila monster!"

I cringed. *Gila* was the Malay word for "insane." Sure, it was common slang in those days, especially when a person didn't like your behaviour or what you had to say, but still. It didn't stop me from feeling terribly embarrassed that my new classmate likened me to a venomous lizard. I imagined my tongue sticking out, coated with poison, hanging down to the ground.

"What? Seen a *hantu*?"

"Oh, sorry." My face felt hot. Worse and worse.

"Don't be stupid. My father's Malay and my mother's a Nonya. Get it?"

"I'm mixed too."

"Mixed or mixed up?" She winked at me.

"I mean, I'm like you." Heat from my blush spread down my face and neck.

"Like me and not like me. You better not assume. Okay?" She wagged a finger at me, with an exaggerated pout on her face.

As the months went by, I got to witness more instances of Faridah's direct manner. She excelled in our English literature class. She also liked Math and Physics, my two weakest subjects. Biology and English were my favourites, although I felt rather inferior in my English skills when I compared myself to my friend. I had a tendency to mix up words that had sounds or syllables in common, which sometimes got me into trouble. Biology, on the other hand, gave me a means to associate words with images, which somehow reduced the confusion. I loved drawing the insides of plants, their secret structures so astoundingly ordered and elegant.

We were the two tallest girls in class and sat at the very back of the room, our desks separated by a two-foot aisle, just enough space for the teacher to walk through.

"My father doesn't want me to mix with boys too early," she once whispered to me across our aisle. "He's very protective of me," she proclaimed with noticeable pride in her subdued voice.

"I don't care about boys," I offered back.

"Late bloomer. Just you wait!" she whispered emphatically, her hand over one side of her mouth.

OUR form mistress, Miss Rajah, was also our English literature teacher. At eighteen, she was a mere five years older than her students. We were the first class she ever taught.

One day, in the middle of our school year, Miss Rajah made a surprising announcement: "Girls, I want to discuss a project for all of us. It's something we will perform for the end-of-year school concert."

I looked up at Miss Rajah, sitting on top of her desk, cradling *Henry V* in her hands.

"How many of you have heard of 'Desiderata'?"

Silence. No hands up.

"Oh, okay . . ."

At that point, the bell for recess rang, and we stood up and boomed in unison, "Thank you, Miss Rajah!"

"Class, after recess, I'll show you the 'Desiderata' text and we can talk about plans to practise it."

Faridah and I ran off to the tuck shop to look for the *kachang puteh* man who sold fried and steamed pulses. After we bought our snacks, we went to the back of the dentist's hut behind the school. It was away from where the other girls liked to hang out, and gave us some privacy.

We sat down to our snacks. We only had thirty minutes before class resumed.

I was eating steamed chickpeas. I loved feeling their skin peel off between my fingers as I pressed against each chickpea. The naked legume gleamed all shiny and smooth in the sun. I popped one into my mouth and continued to do the same with every one of them. Before long, I had accumulated a small mound of their skins on the pavement next to me.

"Aiyah! Gross," exclaimed Faridah. *"Cheena bukit."*

I flushed with anger. "Why are you calling me *cheena bukit?*" It was an insult. This term conjured up an image of a Chinese man descending from the hills, ignorant and possessing crude habits. How dare she lump me in with coolies and rough men who lived sleazy lives in Chinatown and slept with prostitutes! I thought of my Kong-Kong, how he was part of that generation of men who came to Singapore.

"Just joking! Look at your face! Red. What's the matter?"

"Don't make fun of me. I come from a good background. Kong-Kong was a merchant's son, from the upper class, not coarse like *cheena bukit*. He even has an English name!"

"Oh yeah?"

I straightened up from my slouch and recited, *"Faith is a myth and beliefs shift like mists on the shore."*

"What?"

"Joseph Conrad. Kong-Kong named himself Conrad after the famous writer."

"Impres*sive*." She emphasized the last syllable, giving it a Singlish twist.

"I'm a true Singaporean. Just like you." But that knot in my gut hadn't disappeared, and I cast my eyes down at the concrete.

"Why get angry so easily? Don't be so serious, lah!" Faridah gave me some of her deep-fried lima beans as a peace offering.

I looked at her dejectedly, but popped some lima beans into my mouth. Their salty crunch was a pleasant contrast to the steamed chickpeas.

I studied her profile. Regal nose, long eyelashes, big, deep-set eyes. By that time, I had learned that her father, Osman, although mostly of Malay heritage, was proud to have some Arabic ancestry. I recalled pictures I had seen in storybooks, drawings that illustrated *One Thousand and One Nights*. *Faridah is much more beautiful than Scheherazade*, I thought.

I followed her gaze and looked out at the wide field shared by three schools: Haig Girls' Primary, Haig Boys' Primary and ours, Tanjong Katong Girls' School. The field was deserted; the air, heavy and still. I took out my hankie and wiped sweat off my neck. I stuck out my lower lip and blew a stream of air upward, directing the breeze to my forehead. The school bell rang to signal the end of recess.

"Let's go," I said, getting up.

When we returned to the classroom, Miss Rajah had just finished filling the blackboard with large cursive letters, done with yellow chalk.

"Welcome back, class," she said, pausing as all thirty-six of us noisily shuffled back to our seats, the metal legs of our chairs and desks making squeaks and thuds against the concrete floor.

"This is 'Desiderata.'" She tapped the blackboard with the tip of her chalk. "Don't worry about copying it out. The office is making cyclostyled copies. They'll be ready by tomorrow."

Miss Rajah made us read out the text in unison, but try as we might, our recital was discordant and out of sync. Like waves of voices crashing into one another. I didn't mind. It was the first time I had ever been a part of a group of people reading something that had nothing to do with church. It made me feel serene.

"Rumour has it this was an old text discovered in a church, written many years ago. But remember, girls, just because we read it somewhere, doesn't mean it's for sure."

Giggles erupted through the classroom. I sat up from my slouch, impressed by our teacher's healthy skepticism.

Miss Rajah continued, "Regardless, it's a moving piece of writing that would lend itself well to a public performance. I'll bring in the recorded version, and we'll model ours on it."

"Why have you chosen this piece, Miss Rajah? It's so

hippie ... so *ang mo*." Faridah could hardly contain her disdain, placing emphasis on the Hokkien term we all knew, the name for Westerners in general that literally meant "red-furred beasts."

"The peace movement is nothing to be smirked at, young lady. 'Desiderata' seems apropos, given the reality of the Vietnam War."

"Okay, but why use something foreign when we could use something local?"

"Like?"

"How about something by Confucius or ... some such sage," I ventured hesitantly.

"A fine idea. Except it would be nice to have something that crossed the cultural divide, something not limited to one culture or historical context."

"I get it. Something with universal appeal."

"That's right, Natalie," Miss Rajah nodded and beamed at me.

After school, Faridah and I walked along Tanjong Katong Road, pausing outside Will's confectionery. We made loud sniffing noises to show the owners that we enjoyed the fragrance of their freshly baked chicken pies, replete with the buttery smell of onions and crackling puff pastry.

We turned right onto Dunman Road and settled into a leisurely pace. As I looked up at the tall coconut trees flanking the wide, double-lane road, I noticed a Malay youth climbing one of the trees, shimmying up like a monkey. A rubber sling around his waist hugged the trunk, and along his back, tucked into his trouser belt, was a parang. I shuddered, imagining its sharp edge. An image of those men wielding parangs that frightening day in Geylang Serai in July 1964 flashed through my mind.

The youth paused halfway up the coconut tree and leaned against the rubber sling to keep it taut against his body. I was impressed. Despite my initial nervousness, I felt a rush of joy from watching him.

"Don't you wish you could do that?" I asked Faridah.

"No, of course not. My parents would never allow their daughter to do such a risky thing."

"Sure wish I could," I sighed.

When we got to Joo Chiat Road, I said to Faridah, "Do you want to come into the shop?" After a few months of walking home along the same route, I had finally plucked up the courage to invite her in.

Faridah looked a little wary, staring at the impressive sign above Cosmic Pulse. "Maybe another time. Got to get home."

Reluctant to say goodbye, I walked a little further with her, along Koon Seng Road.

We strolled past a row of narrow semi-detached houses, set quite far back from the pavement. I especially admired two that stood right next to each other. They boasted ornate designs of flowers and birds under the eaves and all down the pillars. Gaudy. They reminded me of Mah-Mah's sarongs. Flowers and birds were painted in glaringly bright colours: green for the flowers, yellow for their centres and pink for the birds. Not like real life. Maybe that's why I liked those houses: theirs were the liveliest façades, compared to their neighbours', which looked shoddy and rundown. They were lonely, precisely because they dared to stand out. From that day on, I thought of them as the Lonely Twins.

When we reached Everitt Road, I said goodbye and headed back to the shop while Faridah continued toward Joo Chiat Close.

I stepped into Cosmic Pulse. Kong-Kong was nowhere to be seen. Hwi's back was turned to me as he copied down some instructions while standing at one of the pull-out wooden counters, elbows gingerly poised on the temporary table. Mah-Mah and Uncle were having words at the back of the store. I could hear their voices coming from her special room. I tiptoed quietly toward the room and peered in, past the indigo curtains that hung over the entrance.

"I want extra money," Uncle said, the muscles in his jaw twitching as he spoke.

As soon as I heard her low, soft voice say no, I made as much noise as I could in the corridor. Stomping my feet and clearing my throat loudly. Uncle turned around and stormed out, brushing past me.

Mah-Mah smiled warmly at me. That was enough of a thank you. Sometimes we knew how to say things to each other without speaking. She lowered her head, staring at the wooden disks on her embroidered silk scarf. She soon fell into a trance.

I knew enough to leave Mah-Mah alone when she was in one of those states. I entered the courtyard, where Mum was squatting as she tended to the pot of food cooking over the charcoal stove. I recognized the tangy fragrance of my favourite food and peered into the pot to confirm it. "Braised pig trotters with *assam* seasoning and dried chilies." I licked my lips appreciatively.

"Just like a dog!" Mum quipped. "This food for dinner. Quick, wash your feet."

I took off my white socks and canvas shoes and scooped water from the well, pouring it slowly over my feet. I smiled with pleasure at the sensation of my whole body cooling down. Clogs on, I clunked upstairs, two steps at a time, shoes and socks in one hand and school-bag in the other.

I passed by my parents' bedroom and caught sight of Papa sleeping. Why was he home so early in the afternoon? He was usually at work until six o'clock.

After dropping my things in my room, I went back downstairs.

Mum was now sitting on a low stool, plucking the ends off bean sprouts and placing the trimmed sprouts in a flat enamel dish. I sat down on another stool next to her and helped.

"No extracurricular today?"

"No. How come Papa home early?"

"Too tired. Don't worry. Eat lunch."

I ate a cheese and cucumber sandwich that Mum had

fixed for me, watching her stir the delicious-looking stew. After lunch, I went back upstairs. I shivered from the eerie silence.

In my room, I flung *Henry V* onto the bed, then quickly slipped under the bed. This was my favourite place to be when I needed to think about something particularly sensitive or private. I pretended that being under the bed made me invisible. No one could find me, stop me thinking, however weird my ideas. I glanced at three dust bunnies congregating at the far corner.

Why was Papa home so early? Wasn't he doing the rounds of clinics and hospitals in Jurong today? I thought of how Papa had changed over the years. I hadn't forgotten the Papa who had been cheerful at home. There were photographs to prove it. Photos couldn't lie. I especially liked the ones Mum had taken of him lying on the bed and lifting me up in the air. I was a baby then, couldn't have been more than one. I looked cute in diapers made from Mah-Mah's old sarong. What happened to that happy father who took delight in me? Someone sucked the joy from that man and chucked it into the *longkang* drain, the filthy water swiftly transporting Papa's precious spirit away. What remained was this grumpy fellow who spent an excessive amount of time with squishy Akai headphones on, listening to recordings of church music. His favourite LP was a rare record of Nat King Cole singing Christian hymns. That was how I got to be called Natalie. Papa used to tell me I should feel grateful, and hence enjoy the record, but it sure felt unnatural being in-debted to a piece of vinyl.

Papa never asked me about school. It was Mum who did that. Didn't he want to know? The Papa that every-one else knew, in church or at his work, was an enter-taining man, full of humour and pleasantries. But the person we lived with was sullen, unhappy.

The night before, after Mum went to bed, Papa had snuck into my room and lain next to me. His breath stunk. As always, I pretended to be sound asleep. He squirmed around, making his usual grunting sounds.

Even though this time he didn't make me touch him, the skin behind my ears heated up so much that it soon became unbearable. For the first time in years, ever since Papa started this nauseating nighttime habit, I sat up abruptly. I felt a strong, overwhelming fire rise up from my belly and move outward, right up to my fingertips. This heat possessed my hands and made them push force-fully against Papa's flabby torso. He fell off my bed with a loud thud. Before he could do anything, I jumped out and ran into their bedroom. Mum's eyes were tightly shut in sleep, her arms and legs wrapped around her blue bolster. I crawled into bed to lie next to her. I heard his footsteps, creaking the floorboards outside.

He must have slept on our narrow sofa all night.

It was the first time I'd ever retaliated. The first time I'd ever fought back. I felt powerful. Anger was going to free me.

Under the bed, thinking about what had happened the night before, I vowed that I would never love anyone. I couldn't help but love Papa when I was a baby. How could I have known he was going to turn out to be so sick with me? That's the problem when you're young: you're just too vulnerable. But now that I knew, I promised myself I would grow up to be someone who wouldn't let anyone get that close. Just in case they were going to turn on me.

My fingers felt itchy again, and I scratched, careful not to get carried away. They didn't flare up as much these days, compared to when I was six. Like that time when Papa came home on Chinese New Year's Eve and threatened to snip my fingers off. I shuddered from the memory.

I tucked my hands under my head and sighed. I poked at the dust bunnies with my toes. They didn't like being disturbed. I tried to remember some of the lines from "Desiderata." The phrase that appealed to me the most was "remember what peace there may be in silence." *Yeah, that is so true*, I thought, as I lay there, feeling the cool wooden planks against my arms and legs. I stretched my body and shivered with relief.

The next day, Saturday, we made our usual outing to Bugis Street just as dusk was approaching. We stepped off the bus and walked through the quiet side streets toward the heart of the *pasar malam*, the night market. The alluring glimmer of lights ahead beckoned to us. We stopped first to eat some wonton noodles topped with succulent barbecued pork slices, caramelized sugar darkening the outer edges. It wasn't much of a surprise any more, the chilling silence between my parents. I made lip-smacking sounds, then licked my fingers, trying to draw them out with my antics. Mum and Papa seemed oblivious to me. They didn't seem to care.

I soon gave up and become moody myself. My parents' silence was definitely not the kind meant in "Desiderata." It was far more unbearable than their out-and-out shouting episodes.

I was glad when we finally reached the market. We were surrounded by countless glittering objects. Toys and clothes, kitchen gadgets, cheap watches all laid out on long tables with slanted display stands, while housecoats, pyjamas and lingerie hung overhead on wire hangers. Mandarin love songs blared from oversized speakers under the glare of naked light bulbs: "I'm waiting, waiting for you, but you don't return. I'm waiting, waiting."

I held onto Mum's hand and pulled her toward everything that caught my attention. I didn't notice until much later that Papa was no longer anywhere to be seen.

"Where's Papa?"

"Gone."

"What?"

"Home, that's all."

Mum refused to look at me but squeezed my hand very tight. I saw a tear trickle down her face from her left eye. She plucked her hankie from her beaded handbag and dabbed the tear away. She sniffed at the knot tied at one corner of the hankie, scented with 4711 Eau de Cologne. Then she mumbled to no one in particular, "No one knows how much I suffer. And what for?"

"What for?" I echoed.

"For you, that's what. Means you have to be good girl, Natalie. You can't give me anything to worry about, because Mum has too hard a life, and now too late for me. You mustn't disappoint me, daughter."

I didn't know what to say. It hurt in my chest to hear that she was suffering for my sake. But I was suffering too, and why didn't she know it? On top of all that, I had to make it up to her. But how could I? Our family life was surely far worse than *General Hospital* or *Days of Our Lives*. More twisted than any soap opera. I cast my eyes at the *ah kua*, the men dressed up as women, in their glamorous sequined *cheongsams* and heavy makeup. They were singing enthusiastically, their hoarse yet tender voices competing with the speaker music. Belting out a medley of Beatles tunes: "Hey Jude," "Yesterday," "Norwegian Wood" and lastly "Something." I gawked at the flashy performers. They must have some secrets too, just like me. Yet they acted so cheery. Maybe this was the way I had to make it up to my mother. I nudged Mum to look. "See? So pretty!" I said, with a forced smile.

"Don't look! Shameful." She dragged me away, down the next aisle of stalls.

I started to cry too, feeling confused. No one around could tell me what the truth was, how I could fix the rifts that existed in my family. I ached inside, but there was no one I could talk to. I stared at the faces around us, strangers entranced by the pull of cheap goods.

When Mum and I arrived home, we proceeded to the well in the courtyard to wash our feet. In the dark, the white strips of muslin looked ghostly hanging from the laundry line, slightly stirred by a breeze. The cool water from the well shocked my tired, sticky feet. I looked up through the sky window and caught a glimpse of the moon, full yet veiled by clouds.

Upstairs, the air was stifling. The heat pressed against me like an unwelcome intruder. My parents' bedroom door was closed. I spied the faint light of their table lamp seeping through the gap under the door. Mum went into their room without a further word to me.

I felt restless. As quietly as possible, I switched on the TV, keeping the volume low. Ever since my parents had bought the TV, I hadn't been able to stop watching. I spent every free moment I could in front of it. The last bit of a musical was on Channel 5, our local RTS channel. Fred Astaire was just starting to dance up along the walls and onto the ceiling. Impressive movie trick. His gaunt, angular face beamed happiness.

I turned the knob counter-clockwise to Channel 3, the Malaysian Channel. A large, scaly monster trampled across a city while human beings watched in fright. The monster was much taller than the buildings and swished its long, muscular tail as it moved. It decimated buildings, bridges and towers with a beam emitting from its mouth. On our modest Rediffusion black-and-white screen, the beam looked more like a spray of mist.

I shuddered as I watched the movie. I recognized Raymond Burr from the TV series *Perry Mason*, except he looked a whole lot younger in this movie. All the other characters were Japanese, and the whole movie was dubbed into English. With Malay subtitles.

I sat inches away from the screen so I could hear the sound effects. The dubbing was poor, so the characters' English voiceovers were out of sync with their mouth movements.

I heard enough to figure out what the story was. Godzilla was a monster that lived under the sea off Japan near Odo island, awakened by nuclear testing. He rose from the oceans and trampled and devastated Tokyo with big beams from his mouth that killed people and wreaked havoc on buildings, ships and cars. He destroyed everything that was in his way. Raymond Burr kept showing up in scenes to comment on what was happening. Then there was a hero called Ogata who was determined to destroy the monster, to do whatever was needed. But someone else—an elderly professor—wasn't sure about using a weapon to combat the monster. In the end, the weapon was used, Godzilla destroyed, and Ogata got the girl.

At the end of the movie, I switched off the TV and retreated into my bedroom. I lay at the foot of the bed and clutched my bolster close. My body quaked and broke out into a cold sweat. I clasped my arms tightly around the bolster. Imagined being trampled underfoot by Godzilla. Quick, I had to hide. I slipped down onto the creaky wooden floor. Slid under the bed. Cool and dark underneath. I began to breathe more easily.

I curled my hands into fists and pressed them tightly against my belly. Godzilla's scales made me think of the eczema on my hands. Scales were hard yet brittle. My skin was sometimes like that. It came off my fingers easily in tiny fragments, all foreign-looking and alien from the rest of me.

Godzilla didn't hold back. His rampage all over Tokyo didn't seem personal, because his expression looked pretty much the same throughout the movie. He didn't seem to have any special preference for one kind of destruction or a particular kind of enemy. He simply went berserk. A creature that could deal you a fatal swipe at any moment.

Monsters had to go on rampages. It was inevitable. We humans would survive only if monsters were kept dormant. They're dangerous when awakened and—as Ogata said—you've got to get them before they kill you.

BY THE time I arrived at school on Monday, I had made up my mind.

"Hey, let's go." Faridah beckoned to me to follow her

when the bell rang for recess.

"You go ahead." I gently pressed my hand against the back of Faridah's shoulder.

"Why are you looking so worried?" she asked.

I whispered in her ear, "It's…it's…this movie I saw Saturday night. *Godzilla*. I have to speak to Miss Rajah." I glanced at our teacher. She was seated at the table, marking papers.

After Faridah left, I walked up to Miss Rajah. I stole a look at an examination booklet on the table. The pages my teacher had just marked were filled with her neatly penned comments in red ink. I smiled, relieved to see that it wasn't my booklet.

"Teacher," I began, "did you see the Godzilla movie?"

Miss Rajah looked up from her marking and blinked. "What was that?"

"Godzilla, the big, sick monster. Channel 3, Saturday."

Miss Rajah shut the examination booklet. "Godzilla? You must mean the midnight movie. No, I didn't watch it. You stayed up so late?"

"I've got questions. Would you please help?" I gulped, taking in quick breaths, and shoved my hands into the side pockets of my pinafore. There was a small pebble in the left pocket, and I turned it around again and again with my fingers.

"Why don't we talk about it later? After school. Meet me here at one o'clock and we can have a chat. I have to finish this marking right now."

Just after one, we found a spot outside the staff room, under the large, spreading angsana tree. I knew we had a bit of time, since Miss Rajah's ride usually didn't arrive before 1:20. Every few minutes, a breeze would stir the branches enough to send a squadron of winged pods twirling down around us. The brown pods landed on my crumpled pinafore, collecting in the well of my lap. Miss Rajah seemed oblivious to the flight of the wing-tipped angsana. She looked relaxed, tilting her head to one side as she waited for me to begin.

"About Godzilla . . ." I frowned.

"Yes?"

"In the movie, there's this old professor who said that Godzilla got resurrected because of nuclear experimentation. That the monster was full of atomic radiation. So I think Godzilla must have something to do with the A-bomb. I mean, since it's a Japanese movie. Even though this one has got an American character who pops up once in a while."

"Interesting. You have a question?"

"Yeah. How come we don't have anything in our history syllabus about the atomic bombings of Hiroshima and Nagasaki?"

Miss Rajah's eyes grew wide. Her lips parted slightly as if she was on the verge of saying something. She lifted her right hand slowly and tucked her hair behind her ear. "I don't know the answer to that question for sure, but I suspect it's because of people's feelings. They're not convinced it's a good idea to talk about it in schools yet. Singaporeans of our parents' generation are still bitter about the Japanese occupation of the island. Some Chinese lost relatives during the Nanking Massacre in China. So it was a double blow for those people."

"But, Miss Rajah, two wrongs don't make a right! Those bombs killed a lot of people and scarred others for life." I felt a hot wave pass from my chest up my neck to the spot between my eyebrows. I picked up an angsana pod from my lap and tore open the pulpy, brown exterior to reveal two small red seeds nestled inside.

"Correct. We must never say that violence for the sake of one cause is more justifiable than for another. Evil is evil."

Miss Rajah brought out a roll of Mentos from her humongous sisal bag, stuffed full of textbooks, and offered me one. I popped a sweet into my mouth and crushed it quickly between my teeth. The flavours of lemon and mint filled my mouth.

"Teacher, isn't that what you were thinking of when you mentioned 'Desiderata' and the Vietnam War?"

"What do you mean, Natalie?"

"How can we always make one side the bad guy and the other side the good guy, like they do in the movies? But what does a movie have to do with real life?"

"You're asking another very important question."

I looked askance at my teacher. "Huh?"

"What does art have to do with real life? Is art supposed

to comment on the problems we face? Must art do something more?"

"What more is there to do?" I curled the fingers of my left hand over the angsana seeds, rattling them lightly in the hollow of my palm.

"Make us think. Make us wonder how we can do things differently."

I remembered the line from "Desiderata." "So it's like making peace out of silence?"

Miss Rajah laughed. "That's quite the leap of thought! Now, anything more you want to say about the movie?"

"Maybe Godzilla would have been fine if it weren't for the nuclear accident. People did that to him. I mean, the atomic bomb."

"He's a monster. Of course he's dangerous."

"Is that what a monster has to be? It has no choice but to be mean?"

"Natalie! Look at that furrow between your eyebrows, goodness, lah!" Miss Rajah slapped her thigh as she launched into Singlish to make her point.

I blushed and flapped my pinafore up and down, briskly clearing my lap of the angsana pods. I liked my teacher a lot. With her, I never felt judged or shamed. I never felt that I owed her something or that I had to be someone other than myself. Miss Rajah made school feel the exact opposite of how it felt at home with my parents.

My teacher stared at me and said solemnly, "Still waters run deep. You're a peculiar one, girl."

The blue van pulled up, and the driver honked three times. Miss Rajah got up from the grass and, deftly gathering her books and bag, said goodbye and walked to the van.

seven 脈

"Were you in love with her?" Michelle asks, as we sit facing each other on the bed, under the spell of moonlight streaming through the window.

"I was a teenager. Of course I was."

"Still in love with her?"

I pull myself closer to the window and look out. Quiet on the street. Just before midnight on Sunday. Across from her second-floor apartment on St. Andrew Street, on the side of the yellow brick building, is a lovely graffiti sign welcoming visitors to Kensington Market. And beyond it, to the south, the CN Tower. The moon is full, now almost above the needle-shaped tower.

The image reminds me of the Chinese character for "seduce," the sharp weapon perched suggestively above the mouth. But in the view outside, the image is turned upside down: the voluptuous moon looks ready to mount the phallus, shifting from red in the midsection to purple, with the tip showing a hint of carmine.

I turn back to face Michelle. "That was a long time ago. Besides, it's a stupid phrase, anyway, 'in love.' Just words."

"We need words to make sense of reality."

"Okay, Ms. Librarian."

"Hey, look who's talking. You like poetry."

"Only a few select poems. My tastes are limited."

"Refined, I would say. You doth protest too much, darling." Michelle reaches out to caress my neck and pulls me toward her as she sits back against the headboard.

Directly across from the bed, the small rotary fan futilely circulates the hot air around the room. The aging fan makes a few soulful clunks at either end of its oscillation, but nonetheless provides pleasure through its reliable tempo.

Michelle likes to keep her glasses on. They slip down the low bridge of her nose often, especially in hot weather. This time, I nudge them gently back up with the tip of my tongue.

I reach for the book on the side table, a translation of tanka poems by Akiko Yosano. Opening up *Tangled Hair*, I recite tanka number 35:

Yesterday,
Wondering about

The outcome of my love,
How lonely I was
Even then.

I close the book as a shiver of recognition runs down my back. I'm not sure of myself tonight. Not sure how steady my hands could be. Truth can be rather unpleasant. Yosano's words echo my own state of mind. An independent woman lauded for her tankas, Yosano was unusual for her generation, but even she had felt hopelessly at the mercy of her lover.

How lonely I was, even then.

I return the book to the side table and reach under the bed, lift the coils of hemp rope to my face and inhale. Smells from that other time arrive unbidden. The grassy-sweet smell of jute sacks, their tops rolled down to display the varieties of rice, pulses and dried red chilies. Hemp, like jute, exudes a raw scent, reminds me of the urgency of my needs.

It's imperative never to rush ahead of the one you serve. All strategies in love and war advise us of this. I turn to face Michelle and drop the rope onto the mattress behind her. Sitting cross-legged across from her, I caress her very slowly, up and down the length of her spine, as if I were mulling over a possibility, not quite decided on the approach. My slow deliberation is traced along her back where the yin channels run, hidden to the world, private and receptive.

Michelle wraps her arms loosely around me as we kiss. My hands reach for the rope and position the centre point behind her neck. While kissing her, I gently nudge her face back until the rope makes contact with her nape. She shivers but says nothing. I bring the rope forward on either side of her neck, letting both strands drape down the front of her torso as I pull away slightly and draw her off the bed to stand facing me on the floor.

Tonight I'm going to weave a pattern called The Tortoise. This body harness is one of my favourite shapes. Every time I do this tie, I think of the first tortoises I ever saw, swimming in the pond at Ayer Hitam temple in Penang. I'll loop the ropes instead of knotting them, so there's more give to the harness, more room for Michelle to move around.

I whisper into her neck, "They used to believe that binding the body allowed the soul to be captured."

"Yeah, those bloody torturers, right?" She glances mockingly at me, then continues, "Do you believe that?" Her lips in the dark, lit only by moonlight, seem unearthly.

"No, I don't. One can bind the body, but the soul— whatever that is—can't be captured that easily." I think of the Japanese bad-boy photographer Nobuyoshi Araki, who has said that he bound a woman's body because he knew there was no way he could bind her heart.

"Why do you resist being bound? Does it always have to be the other person?"

I had guessed a day would come when Michelle would

ask me this. Nevertheless, I'm still caught by surprise, and I pause, my finger at Conception Vessel 7, right between her breasts.

She persists. "I want to learn. You know I'd make a good student."

"Shush . . ."

"Why won't you let me?"

"You dare ask, despite the fact that I am your *nawashi*—"

"—who is supposed to be serving me, not withholding information. I think I know the answer."

"Then you tell me . . ."

"You must have tried it, but realized it wasn't for you."

"Maybe . . . maybe not."

She sighs as I pass the two lines of rope between her legs to the back, pulling them taut as I move behind her.

I plant a light kiss on the nape of her neck, just above the rope. "I'll miss you," I say, trying to change the topic.

"You're going to see her soon. You've made all these arrangements at work and at home. In less than a week. That must mean something."

"It means I still care about her."

I insert the ends of my rope through the centre point and under it, just below her neck, making sure I've allowed enough slack. Then the separating of the lines and the single overhand knot over the rope on the spine. I pull the ropes, one under each arm, toward her chest, just above her breasts. She draws in a breath, sharp and definite. It behooves a *nawashi* to quicken her pace when the need arises. I now move twice as fast as the lazy oscillation of the fan. Ropes criss-crossing over vertical lines, then tightened sufficiently to keep them separated.

The shape of a tortoise slowly emerges down her torso. I finish the harness at her thighs. Her body glistens with a shimmer of sweat.

I touch the small of her back, reaching for the place where the ropes meet, and, winding my fingers around them, pull very slowly to tighten the harness, giving her more pleasure as her breasts are pushed up slightly. She isn't shy, offering a well-timed moan of appreciation. I press against the points where portions of the rope intersect.

"Kidney 21...17...14." I press near the sternum, "Conception Vessel 20." Between the breasts, "cv 17..."

"Tell me more."

"cv 8...just above your belly button..."

"Mmm...definitely makes me hungry for more torture."

"Here's cv 2, just two inches above your sex."

"Who knew that acupuncture could be so fun?"

"You should try it. Come to the clinic for the real needles."

She laughs, amused by my pitch.

I whisper into her ear, "Nothing is more compelling than experience, hmm?" Then, quoting Lao Tzu, *What is well embraced cannot slip away.*

I reach down to cv 1, between her legs. I let myself disappear into the rhythm of her breathing, the strong, familiar heave of her torso.

We tumble back onto the bed. Nuit soon scampers into

the room. She hops up and settles next to Michelle just as I'm starting to untie the ropes. Impeccable timing. Her lovely green eyes gaze at us as she places her front paws on Michelle's shoulder.

I turn away from them as I put my clothes back on.

"Natalie, don't get caught up in her world, okay?"

"Hey, don't worry."

"The past can't be changed."

"Of course not."

"You're acting like someone with a debt to pay. You don't owe her anything."

"Yeah, I do."

THE shops in Kensington are closed. The plum-coloured canopy with green and burgundy stripes at the fruit market downstairs has been rolled up for the night. It's slightly past 3:00 a.m., the time of morning when the body is aligned energetically along the lung meridian. According to Traditional Chinese Medicine, it's also when grief manifests most powerfully. Yet the empty streets grant me a rare pleasure. The world has retreated from its show of hectic pretence.

I breathe in the quiet air, feeling the calm spread through me. I feel peaceful. Placated. It's always like this after I do Kinbaku. Before I entered the world of Kinbaku practice, I had all kinds of notions about it, none of them positive. I thought, *It's dark, it's weird, and it hurts.*

There's a notion in Kinbaku that goes like this: by binding the body, the true nature of one's spirit emerges. I've seen that happen with the lovers I've bound. The falling away of the superficial, the shedding of the incidental. But they're brave, unlike me. I'm not sure I have the guts to be that vulnerable.

The risk of being so open. I haven't forgotten the promise I made to myself as a teenager. That I would never let anyone get that close to me.

How could I let Michelle bind me? I'm worried that I might feel something ugly when I'm bound. What if I snap? I don't want that to happen. And maybe I'm also scared that Michelle won't like what gets revealed if I let her bind me.

It's a gamble. The risk, incalculable.

The cool wind soothes my hot forehead as I cross Spadina. I can smell a hint of metal in my sweat. I feel happily connected to a sense of spaciousness: a vast, expansive feeling in the lungs, the neighbourhood opened up through the absence of others. Cleaner air spared the incessant traffic and cigarette smoke of crowded streets.

I pass by Kom Jug Yuen, with the hooks hanging in space, deprived temporarily of roast ducks and barbecued pork.

Taking Cecil Street instead of Baldwin, I pause in front of the community centre's bulletin board, where classes are listed. Mr. Woo's name is there. He's been teaching taiji and qigong ever since his wife passed away.

Mr. Woo has been accepting of Michelle's relationship with me from the very beginning, when we started dating three years ago. Even though Mr. Woo has been a patient of mine for about seven years, I only met Michelle when she came by the clinic to pick up her father one evening in the spring of 2004. Funny how that happens, just when you don't expect it. I was open to Michelle because I already had such a strong connection with her father and had heard lovely things about her. They have such an easygoing relationship. I was struck from the very beginning by how different Michelle's childhood was from mine.

Mum has never referred to Michelle as my lover. But she likes her. She makes me take soup and stews whenever I visit Michelle. I chose not to tell Papa, because I knew how he would react. He wouldn't have accepted it.

Things are different now. Even if he weren't suffering from the consequences of the stroke, nothing he could do or say would carry the power he used to have. He couldn't prevent me from being with someone I love. Not anymore.

I ENTER our townhouse, taking care to walk lightly down the hallway. In the kitchen, the fluorescent clock on the stove reads 3:36 a.m. I switch on the TV and flip channels until I catch the beginning of a Korean movie, *Sympathy for Lady Vengeance*. The credits are suggestively gothic, crimson red ink turning into drips of blood on a pure white cloth.

Even though I'm tired, I can't stop watching. The title character's pale, angelic expressions are chilling as she manifests anger in its coldest and most determined forms. It's a dark twist to restorative justice: Lady Vengeance helps the parents of murdered children take revenge on the killer. She's a Dark Madonna, a Saviour figure driven by pure intent and clear vision. It's an utterly terrifying movie, but oddly entrancing. I think it's because the woman who plays Lady Vengeance makes the character so believable, in all her complexity. Who can't relate to someone who's been horribly wronged? Who doesn't feel an urge to exact revenge? I can't help but like her.

At the end of the movie, I switch off the TV. It's almost dawn, but I don't need to wake up early. I'm no longer sleepy, anyway. Under the sink, next to the pots and pans, behind the bottles of olive oil and soy sauce, is a bottle of Benedictine Dom. I pour myself a small glass. Back in the chair, I put my feet up on the table and lean back as far as I can without tipping over.

Crazy yet brilliant movie. *Sympathy for Lady Vengeance* is neither a simple horror movie nor a conventional thriller. Disturbing because it refuses stereotypes, refuses to divide the world into two basic camps of good and evil. In fact, good and evil exist within each character, as inseparable as yin from yang.

Candour is dangerous. Recognizing complexity is dangerous.

What would Miss Rajah think of this movie? Would she believe that it fulfills the purpose of art, as she defined it?

I take another sip of Benedictine. I can easily conjure up her warmth, as if I had just seen her at school moments ago. I never minded when she laughed at me, or even when she called me peculiar.

I've lived most of my life feeling like a freak, a misfit. Had to pretend lots, had to hide. I don't have many secrets, but the handful I keep remain a burden. Like the ones about Papa. How could I have told Mum? She seemed too fragile to handle what was going on. She desperately needed me to be a good daughter.

And even though I trust Michelle's love for me, I have chosen not to tell her what Papa did to me. I feel lonely all of a sudden. Wishing I had stayed over at Michelle's, rather than come home. To this very lonely house, where I am reminded of my parents' fragilities.

I can never be a good enough daughter. Deep inside me is someone who has always resisted belonging to my parents. I may continue to live with them, do a few dutiful things, keep silence about the skeletons in our family closet, but there are truths about me I will never show my parents. That is the ultimate rebellion, I suppose.

I get up from the chair and leave my glass in the sink. Enough mental machinations. I had better stop resisting going to bed.

At the foot of the stairs, on the small table where we pile our mail and various keys, are several clippings from the *Toronto Star*. Another hobby of Mum's—saving newspaper clippings of bizarre or gory incidents. A clipping bears the headline: Deadly Script of a Ring Legend. The case of the pro wrestler Chris Benoit. Big news for Hogtown these days, one sensationalist crime that's placed in the foreground of a host of violent acts. My mother most definitely has her dark side. She might have liked *Sympathy for Lady Vengeance*.

When I finally climb up our creaky stairs, I hear Papa snoring loudly and Mom's softer breathing, a low but descending arpeggio on the exhalation.

eight 脉

I stare out my window, down to the street below. No kids out at this early hour of the morning. I'm almost finished packing, but I don't feel anything close to being ready.

Mere existing
Sheer dead weight
Only in emptiness does life begin

I think Mah-Mah would have appreciated that ancient Taoist saying. She, for whom the mystical was unquestionable. I close my eyes when I feel sadness tensing up my throat. Wish I hadn't left Singapore before she died.

"All ready, Natalie?"

I turn around to find Mum standing in the doorway, one hand on her hip, the other pressed against the door. She looks at me with concern.

"Almost."

She frowns. "Don't get involved in her affairs, you know."

"Who?"

"Faridah. You two close long ago, but things change, huh?"

"You're sounding like Michelle."

"Don't forget, she married now."

This is the closest Mum has ever come to acknowledging my relationship with Faridah. For years after that relationship ended, I kept wishing my mother would say something to me about it; even the slightest gesture would have been a balm for my bruised feelings. Now that she's able to allude to it, I can't feel anything. Ironic.

"She needs me. She's going through a terrible time."

"You always loyal, Natalie."

I meet her gaze with mine. *Loyalty*, I think, *comes with a high price tag.*

"Hey, you remember how Kong-Kong liked to quote Joseph Conrad? *Faith is a myth and beliefs shift like mists on the shore.*"

"Got what to do with what?"

"Being loyal, but I don't know . . . beliefs can change."

The doorbell. We both jolt at the sudden interruption.

I look out the window. The red Honda. 5:30 a.m., as promised.

"Can you ask Michelle to wait? I'll be down soon."

As soon as Mum starts down the stairs, I reach into my carry-on backpack. Just to make sure it's there. The cloth bundle containing Mah-Mah's treasure: the Oracle book and the twelve wooden chips that accompany it.

BEFORE we immigrated to Canada, my parents decided that we would only allow ourselves one standard carton each of mementoes. Actually, it was Papa's idea. He insisted that we not burden ourselves with too much memorabilia of the past. For him, the box was filled with old records. For Mum, it was a box of family photo albums and ten of her favourite novels by the Taiwanese author Qiong Yao. My box contained one small shadow box of butterflies from Cameron Highlands, my report cards from the three schools I attended, a handful of photos and books, a few toys from childhood and, of course, Mah-Mah's precious Oracle.

She gave the Oracle to me the night before we left the country. In the courtyard behind Cosmic Pulse, we rested on the low stools, knees almost touching. The moon was almost full, bright light streaming through the sky window. Mah-Mah's eyes gleamed with an unusual mirth. I was puzzled; after all, we were leaving soon.

"Don't you need them?" I whispered, feeling very solemn.

"I got another set chips. Don't need book, everything inside." She pointed to her heart.

"Why are you giving this to me?"

"One day you need. Time will come."

"When would that be?" My eyebrows rose in a distinct show of skepticism.

"Patience, granddaughter."

"Why are you looking so happy, Mah-Mah? Aren't you sad to see us go? I don't want to leave."

"Granddaughter, I feel joy. Canada good for you, you see. You grow happy one day. I already told your Mum. Cosmic Pulse follow you. Make Kong-Kong proud."

Kong-Kong had passed away the previous year, yet she spoke as if he were still alive. She sounded confident that I would be happier in Canada, but I was incredulous. How could she think and feel that way, when I didn't have a clue what direction my life would take in that new country?

MICHELLE and Mum are talking downstairs, their voices easily distinguishable, even from my room. It's not just the age difference: my mother's voice is heavily singsong and raspingly loud, whereas Michelle's is low, supple and soft.

I take out the cloth bundle from my backpack and untie the strings. The wooden chips and the booklet tumble out as I upturn the bag. I handle the wooden chips gingerly, turning each over a few times. The chips have the feel of Mah-Mah's hands on their surfaces. I swear I can sense her heat, imagine her wise touch as she worked with them daily in that back room.

On that last night in Singapore before my parents and I left for Toronto, instead of doing a reading for me, Mah-Mah chose to talk about a couple of trigraphs. First, trigraph number 52, Wickedness Excelling. "Single yang in middle overwhelmed by too much yin in Heaven and Earth, Battle. Too much. Oracle say: *When person is solitary and moreover young, how can he initiate anything?*"

I gasped at hearing the words of the Oracle, recalling the circumstances that had led up to me casting the chips for this trigraph. I felt a knot of pain in my gut at the memory.

She paused as she jabbed a confident finger at the lone *zhong* representing humanity in the middle row. "This person here …" she paused yet again, for emphasis, "…must crouch and wait, save energy. Some day, things turn around."

"How can you be so sure, Mah-Mah?"

"This is Tao's nature. Depend on virtue and spirit."

"Whose?"

"You! I talk you. Pay attention. More auspicious time coming. One day you see. But I not around anymore that future time, granddaughter. Not in body. But you remember, my spirit always with you. That why I want you take Oracle. Then I can continue with you."

Tears welled up in my eyes, my chest aching already from the imminent departure. I nodded, and the tears fell unchecked.

She then turned the page to the next trigraph. "*Shen Zhu*, Assistance of the Spirits. Why I show you this one, you think? So you remember, everything change, all the time. Oracle say, *Four ghosts and two shamans bow to one another.* Spirits of Heaven come down, free imprisoned. You see? Two shamans ask spirits help them, so understand this: not ghosts anymore. Become helping spirits. Secret is: you look inside, find strength. Not get confused, outside is outside. Stay inside. Have high principles, not deceive others."

"Motivation is important," I thought out loud.

"Yes. Must honest, no lie, no cheat."

Mah-Mah's intention was clear. She needed to pass on a legacy, wanted me not to forget why trigraph 52 was particularly significant in my life. But, being a Taoist, she also wanted to talk about change. That's why she referred to trigraph 53, where the presence of two figures in the middle row made all the difference, compared to the previous trigraph. There was hope of rescue following the prior surge of wickedness.

After my parents and I moved to Toronto, I kept wishing we could return to Singapore soon.

Three years later, we made our first trip back. For Mah-Mah's funeral. She died of a brain aneurysm, after falling down the back stairs of that grand house on Koon Seng Road. That was just before I began my last year at U of T. Not long after that, my recurring nightmares began.

It's been a whole lifetime since I've looked at the Oracle. Feels a bit strange.

"What are you doing?" Michelle has come upstairs. She

enters my room and glances down at the oracle chips.

"Hey . . . don't tell me . . ." Her eyes widen in surprise as she deduces the meaning of the wooden chips.

"My grandmother's."

"Some kind of divination tool?"

"Similar to the *I Ching*. But simpler to use."

"Packing it along? You're going to use it?"

"Maybe. Feel like taking it with me at least."

"In Borges' *Death and the Compass*, the detective uses the Kabbala to track down the next victim," Michelle offers.

I laugh nervously. "Hey, wait a minute. This was a suicide. No more victims, okay?"

"Well, how about this: you could use it to track down . . . the reasons for the suicide? A whydunit, as opposed to the usual whodunit."

"Trust a librarian to come up with such a clever idea. I'll see what I can do to satisfy your fantasy, dearest."

She sighs. "I'll be feeling quite deprived without you. We'd better get going or you'll miss your flight."

"Wait."

I make her lie on the bed, and I lift her shirt to look at the fine lines across her front from our last Kinbaku session. Lines that remind me of the energies that pulse through her body, inseparable from the wild, irrepressible spirit that I love.

This will have to do for now, I say to myself, keeping the image firmly in my mind.

nine 脈

The large, curved branches of the Flame of the Forest trees on either side of the highway form a protective canopy against the scorching heat. The air-conditioned taxi cruises away from the airport along the expressway for about fifteen minutes before turning onto the East Coast Parkway. I turn around in the back seat to watch the majestic trees recede into the distance.

The journey on the highway feels abrupt, too quick to allow my mind to acclimatize to the fact that I've arrived in Singapore. Before I know it, the taxi turns off at the exit for Marine Parade Housing Estate. At the traffic lights, a group of schoolgirls in lapis blue pinafores and sharp white blouses trudge in the direction of the nearby library.

I recognize the school uniform. It feels as if it were only yesterday that I viewed Katong Convent girls with a mix of curiosity and wariness. After all, those of us from Tanjong Katong Girls' School had a reputation for being nerdy, while the KC girls were considered more *hiau*, more fun.

I turn away momentarily from the passenger window as the taxi turns into Joo Chiat Road. The sunlight is strong, so brilliant that it hurts to look out. Must be searing hot outside, judging from the squinting expressions of pedestrians, and the generous use of umbrellas to shield against the sun.

I step out of the taxi in front of Hotel 81. For a few minutes, I'm rooted to the spot as I stare up at the hotel, at the familiar block of former shop houses, now restored and occupied by completely different businesses. Hotel 81's outside walls are a light powder blue, while the sculpted bas-reliefs have been painted bone white. To the left of Hotel 81 are a karaoke bar and an Internet café, probably owned by the hotel. Followed by the boarded-up ruins of the next two shop houses: what had been the Lims' provision shop, and Cosmic Pulse next to it. Back in Toronto, while checking out hotels on the web, I had guessed that Hotel 81 was in the same stretch as Kong-Kong's former shop. But I had forgotten the address of Pulse, had no idea it was this close by.

I look up at the rooms above what used to be Pulse. Shutters closed, in shabby shape. Just under the eaves, ferns and various small plants proliferate. I sigh, feeling disconcerted, and drag my two bags into the lobby.

My room upstairs is modest, with a queen-sized bed that takes up most of the small space. A narrow counter to the left of the door displays a coffee maker, packets of Earl Grey tea, Nescafé instant coffee, Coffee-mate and sugar, as well as two polystyrene cups of instant noodles. A sleek TV monitor floats in the opposite corner, perched on a bracketed shelf just below the ceiling. The washroom floor is tiled, the same tiny grey tiles running along the walls up to the level of a single window. No stall to separate the shower from the toilet—typical of the old-fashioned washrooms of the '70s.

I fix myself a Nescafé. The aroma is familiar from the days when Papa drank it every morning before going off to work. I add some Coffee-mate, missing the taste of condensed milk, sit on top of the bed with cup in hand, sipping slowly, trying to collect my thoughts. It's 5:45 p.m. here, which means 5:45 a.m. in Toronto, twelve hours behind Singapore. Couldn't sleep much on the flight over. No wonder I'm tired. I'll need a nap. But not before I call Faridah.

She picks up after only the first ring. "Hello?"

"It's me. Natalie."

"I was wondering when you would call!" There's a slight lilt to her voice. She sounds glad to hear from me.

I keep the conversation brief. Too disoriented from jet lag to think clearly. I make arrangements to meet Faridah

at 7:30 p.m. Shut the blinds and turn on the air conditioning before I pass out on top of the bed.

MORE refreshed after the nap, I walk along Joo Chiat, heading toward East Coast Road. It's just past seven o'clock. The
light is fading, street lamps starting to come on. I recognize
some remnants of the old neighbourhood. Every sensation seems sharper. I feel attentive and vigilant, aware of
traces of the familiar, along with their disappearance.

It takes only ten minutes to reach the *kopi tiam*. Noisy
at this corner of Joo Chiat Road and East Coast Road,
thronging with traffic and punctuated by loud voices.
Probably noisier since it's Friday night.

I choose a table outside the coffee shop. There's an occasional breeze that nonetheless feels unsatisfying. The
humid air coats my skin with a layer of unease. Maybe
it's this very sensation that's making everything seem
more acute.

At the next table are a couple of young Chinese men
with their female companions. Cantopop flows out from
the radio behind the beverage vendor. Sounds like Jacky
Cheung, but it's not a song I know.

I order a Tiger beer. The man at the beverage stall scans
the bar code on the can before bringing it over. He has an
untidy mass of dyed red-orange hair that spills over his
forehead, partially blocking his eyes. Punk rocker look.
He's probably close in age to Faridah and me. Guess it's

never too late to break out.

My can of beer is half empty when I see Faridah walking toward me, dressed in a beige tunic blouse over a long skirt, almost down to her ankles. Her open-toed sandals are rather showy, the row of decorative stones drawing one's attention to the top of each foot.

"Liver 3," I mumble to myself, thinking of the acupuncture point for treating anxiety. My heart starts to beat faster. Faridah's appearance hasn't changed much from the last time I saw her in 2005. A few wrinkles around the eyes and the rare white hair. Surprisingly, no signs of artificial colouring in her hair. But she looks drawn, grief showing in her eyes and the way she carries her body.

"Hello, Nat." She forces a smile as she stands there awkwardly.

I stand up and move toward her, give her a quick hug. She barely responds, her arms limply touching my back before we pull apart. I catch the sweet, heavy scent of jasmine and sandalwood.

I'm amazed to find that the feeling of attraction still exists.

We order bowls of Katong laksa from a stall at the other end of the coffee shop and sit back down.

"I can see ..." I begin, but quickly stop myself. What's the point of saying the obvious? Her grief is frighteningly visible.

Her voice is strained. "It feels strange, meeting under these circumstances."

The two men and their female companions are getting rowdy, the men drinking Guinness and the women picking prawns and squids off steaming plates of Hokkien *mee*, fried noodles that were a favourite meal in childhood. I stare past the revellers at the brisk pedestrian traffic. The rhythms around me are chaotic, full of the unspoken throb of desire and anxiety.

"You won't blame me for being preoccupied with Selim, will you?"

"Of course not. Completely understandable."

"The way I found him . . ." Her eyes redden instantly, and her lips quiver.

I reach out and place my hand on hers while she cries quietly. After a few moments, she gently takes her hand away and wipes her eyes.

"I'm feeling quite mixed up," she whispers, looking down at the ground below the table. "I wanted you to come, and now that you're here, I just don't know what to say. What I need from you. What you can give me."

"Don't think too much about it right now. Just take it easy on yourself."

"I miss our friendship so terribly. I've never dared to speak to you candidly all these years since . . ." Her voice trails off as she starts to cry again, using her hankie to wipe the tears. She doesn't seem to care that her mascara is running.

"Faridah, maybe it hurts too much to talk right now. A lot of emotion from meeting again. Especially under these circumstances." I clear my throat and stare at the table surface, wondering about the feelings people have to suppress in order to coast through their daily activities.

We eat in silence, in contrast to the customers at the next table, who are now ordering another round of Guinness. When we've finished eating, I suggest, "Why don't we take a walk?"

She looks up at me, somewhat surprised. "Where?"

"What about the back streets in the Joo Chiat area? You lead the way."

We walk along Joo Chiat, heading back in the direction of Cosmic Pulse. I can still conjure up some of the old sites. A red building where the community centre now stands. It was the library I frequented as a child. The place I first encountered Dr. Seuss and *Green Eggs and Ham*. Farther down, there was a bakery on the other side of the street that produced hot, fragrant buns topped with big chunks of rock sugar. The bakery is still there, although I can't smell the same kind of baking.

I feel rather odd walking next to her. Seems intimate and distant at the same time. I have an urge to take her hand, not so much out of lust but because I yearn to connect with the love that existed between us. It's the friendship I most long for. We walk in silence. I wonder if she's also remembering our days as teenagers.

Joo Chiat is a much wider street now, throbbing with bars and nighttime eating places. I notice the closed doors of the daytime shops. Hardware supplies, bicycle shop, teak furniture. I count two massage joints. One of them looks sleazy, the other not. It's easy to spot the difference, the former with the vague name "Massage" in squiggly neon yellow letters, while the latter has photos of how Thai massage is conducted and calls itself a Health Centre. There's a lot of neon signage on both sides of the wide street. Bars, massage, karaoke. Suddenly, it clicks.

"Hey, has Joo Chiat become a bit of a red-light district?"

"Yes, unfortunately," she confirms.

"Still living in the same place?"

"Yes."

We turn onto a side street. Some of the houses are rather rundown, narrow like the shop houses on Joo Chiat, but most are private residences. Doors and metal gates locked for the night. Slivers of light filtering through gaps in the wooden shutters over windows. We pass the dark shadow of a temple, incense smoke wafting up from the urn just inside the locked outer gates.

"Hey, can we walk down Koon Seng?" I suggest.

"Sure . . . that's heading in the direction of home for me . . ." She sounds hesitant.

Koon Seng Road, in contrast to Joo Chiat, is very quiet, with hardly any traffic. In this serene atmosphere, the sounds of laughter mixed with sounds of TV emerge from one of the charming Straits Settlement houses. Loud clash of mah-jong tiles being shuffled. A dog barks wildly as we pass in front of its territory.

"Wait a minute," I say, touching Faridah's elbow lightly.

I recognize them, despite the signs of aging. We're in front of the Lonely Twins. They stand side by side, well weathered and sombre. Their painted façades are flaking. They've lost their previous flamboyance, but in place of showiness is a mellow dignity.

"Do you remember them?" I ask Faridah.

"Yes, I remember how much you liked them," she answers, her voice surprisingly tender.

I didn't expect it would be this hard, walking the familiar route home with Faridah. We're no longer those two girls full of hopeful longing. How naive we were. Even me, with all I had to deal with in my family. Didn't I tell myself I wouldn't let anyone get too close? But then there was Faridah.

We reach the place where my grandparents' house used to be. I gasp and step back as I take in the sight of what now occupies the property.

"Hadn't you seen this? It's the new Haig Girls' School."

"Wow, no way. The one that used to be kitty-corner from TKGS."

"That's right. Government has been moving schools to different sites over the years. TKGS has been also moved."

"Good grief. I had no idea. I didn't want to come back to this area. Ever since Mah-Mah passed away."

"How about when you returned in 2005?"

"We stayed with my father's relatives in Toa Payoh."

"You weren't ready to face this before."

"Until now."

I stare at Haig Girls' School, a huge building with smooth, high walls. It stands where Zion Presbyterian Church used to be. Where my grandparents' home and their neighbours' house were, there's a basketball court instead. I peer through the metal gates. By the light of the street lamp, I can make out the school emblem displayed on an outside wall: *Ars Potens Est*, Knowledge is Power.

After Mah-Mah passed away, Uncle wasted little time in closing Cosmic Pulse. Mum was angry when she heard that her brother had done that and sold off the property, squandering the money on gambling and who knows what else. Mum told me recently that Uncle also sold the Koon Seng Road house; she refused to tell me more. I don't know where Uncle has gone, if he's even alive.

It's one thing to hear news indirectly, another to be standing here and experiencing the truth.

I'm not sure how much time passes. It's as if I've forgotten that Faridah is standing there next to me. I'm roused by the awareness of a change in the air. A strong wind shakes the trees overhead.

Faridah speaks up, "How are your parents?"

I was dreading this question. "Oh. My mother's okay, but..."

She looks at me quizzically, waiting.

"My father suffered . . . a stroke. Shortly after we left Singapore in 2005. He—" I stop abruptly, surprised by the wavering in my voice. Caught off guard by the emotions choking me up.

Faridah falls silent again. The wind stirs our clothes.

"I'm very sorry. How awful for you and your mother."

My chest tightens. I feel panicked. What if I lose it, in front of Faridah? It would be horrible. Can't bear the thought. Can hardly breathe. I take my pulses on the right hand, then the left. My lung, spleen and kidney pulses are weak, detectable only when I apply the deepest pressure.

I feel beads of sweat forming on my forehead and between my eyes.

"Are you okay?"

"It's just a passing feeling. Must be the exhaustion. I'll be okay."

"Hey, I need to get back soon," Faridah murmurs.

"Let me walk you home."

We head down Everitt Road toward Joo Chiat Close.

"Remember? Used to be a small *kampong* at this location. This is long before we met. Every time I passed by, I would lean toward the huts, ignoring Ah See's attempts to restrain me, pulling on my sleeve."

"Childhood, a carefree time," Faridah quips.

"Nonsense. But I have a few good memories."

"How unsentimental of you."

"Having too many memories is a distinct disadvantage. Memories can hurt." My chest tightens further as a dull pain spreads over it.

She gasps. The street lamp shines down on us, showing up the startled look on her face.

I should apologize. After all, my friend has just lost her son. But I feel an edge of bitterness surfacing tonight.

She says nothing in response but continues walking, at a quicker pace. I keep up.

We soon reach Joo Chiat Close. Across from us, a row of newly renovated Peranakan homes stretches out. They're very similar to the Lonely Twins, except given new life through transformation. Exquisitely beautiful and minimalist, a soft white framed by dark wooden windows and doors. Looking at these, you could forget there's such a thing as deterioration and aging. We make a left and reach the building where Faridah, Adam and Christina live. On the ground floor is a coffee shop, fronted by a vendor selling *bak chang*, Nonya rice dumplings. Two floors up is their apartment. The lights are on.

"Rest well," I say, feeling awkward. "Can we meet tomorrow?"

"Can't, until Monday. We have some family things to do. Sorry."

"Monday, then."

"I'll call." She doesn't look back as she unlocks the metal gate, then the downstairs door.

I head back toward the hotel. When I pass the location where the *kampong* used to be, I recall early memories of that Malay village. I had wanted to join the children playing games with *goli*, their marbles clashing spectacularly with one another on the dusty ground. Wanted to learn how to work those *gasing* tops; I envied how well the boys could set the wooden shapes spinning, lift them with the string and balance them as they twirled in mid-air.

That *kampong* smelled of freshly ground chilies, curry powder, lemon grass and shallots fried in peanut oil. I loved the sound of scraping claws on sand as the proud rooster and his bevy of hens strutted through the village, creating tiny swirls of dust. *Kampong* life seemed rich with mysteries that eluded me, simply because I wasn't allowed access to that inner world. It was a way of life I didn't understand.

It was the way the early Malay natives lived, long before Raffles arrived in Singapore. The Malays were devoted to that tradition for a long time: to be close to the land, or be fisherfolk. But then there was the unavoidable lure of progress, the various incentives to surrender their former way of life and integrate into urban existence. It became quite impossible to do otherwise.

I don't want to romanticize the former ways, of *kampong* life for Malay villagers. It must have been accompanied by a great deal of hardship. But even then, in my childlike innocence, I sensed there was another direction that life could have taken.

Of those early days, I also remember how keenly I used to struggle with Ah See whenever she tried to drag me away. I was too young to think much of it, simply saw it as Ah See doing her job. After all, she was paid to do things like that, get me back home without any detours.

I think about it differently now. I wonder if Ah See's behaviour was typical among the Chinese populace during the mid- to late '60s in Singapore. The race riots of 1964 led the Chinese to feel nervous around Malays for a long time. I was not supposed to get too close.

I head toward Joo Chiat Road, thinking of the feelings that had erupted earlier when I was with Faridah. I wish I hadn't been so insensitive. For a few moments, I felt out of control. Anger about what Papa did, still there. Distress about Faridah leaving me, thirty-two years ago, still not gone. Coming back to Singapore, like going back in time. Except that now I feel possessed by a persistent edge of bitter disappointment.

I walk up to the boarded-up entrance of what used to be Cosmic Pulse and peer between the cracks into a well of darkness. I inhale the musty, dank smell of ruin. My mind projects back in time, back in space, to the life I led behind the shop, out in that courtyard and in the rooms above. I stare at the decrepit state of the wooden windows above.

Did I fabricate the creatures that materialized in the reflection in the large, rectangular well? What if they really existed? And if so, did Mah-Mah know about them?

I hadn't wanted to confront the loss of Cosmic Pulse until now. All those other visits back to this country, I had avoided this moment. I hate not being able to escape.

Back in my hotel room, I open a can of Tiger beer from the bar fridge and switch on the TV. The Chinese channel is screening *Bu Liao Qing*, *Love Without End*, the movie with the famous sad song "Wang Bu Liao." Mum loved this film. She would beg Papa to take her to the cinema whenever it screened. It was so popular that there would be at least three screenings a year in Chinatown in the years following its initial release. Those were the days when you depended on public screenings to see your favourite films. That was the era of limited access, unlike the current global atmosphere of Internet downloads, DVDs and YouTube.

A film like *Love Without End* was precious precisely because there were few like it. For my mother, in a life that was fraught with regret, this movie voiced what she dared not express. The way she cried over this movie is the most eloquent expression of sadness and regret I've ever encountered.

Yet I've never watched the whole movie from start to finish. Even though I have the song on my iPod. It was almost as if I would not allow myself that indulgence as long as Mum was watching. As if only one of us had permission to need this movie. I laugh quietly at myself. Despite my determination to stay aloof, and the constant cynic in my head making snide comments as I watch, I cry anyway. Lin Dai is the beautiful woman who's crushed by her lover's betrayal, her selfless sacrifice for him completely misunderstood and vilified. The crass cruelty he's capable of is infuriating. And yet, I can see the vulnerability beneath his actions. He too must have felt betrayed.

After switching the TV off, I feel overcome with a heaviness that sits in my gut. The problem with that guy was that he wasn't really open to Lin Dai's love. What a fool he was. Too bloody full of himself, had all kinds of wrong ideas about her. That's what made him vulnerable.

So. To be closed is to be vulnerable. Openness and vulnerability—these aren't the same thing, after all. I had equated them all my life. Fair enough. Ask most women and I bet they would say the same thing. It's a mistake, though. To be open affords an ability to take in all kinds of evidence about life, about what's happening in the here and now. Without openness, how could anyone live fully in the present, respond to what is actually happening, as opposed to things of the past? Instead of seeing what we want to believe, we would stand a chance of seeing what is really here. Right in front of our eyes.

I feel a bit queasy. Dizzy. I lie face down on the bed and let the tears come. Why hold back? What's the point? I don't want to anymore.

I MUST have fallen asleep. When I wake up, I notice it's an hour later. A bit groggy. I make myself another cup of Nescafé. So what if it's late? I need to snap out of this stupor. Time to call home. It's just past 10:00 a.m. in Toronto. It only takes a few rings before Mum picks up.

"How are you, Mum?"

"What time there?"

"Past ten at night. You always forget, it's twelve hours' difference now, before daylight savings time. How's everything?"

"Okay. Strange here, without you. Yesterday Mr. and Mrs. Chan came. Brought *char siew bau*, one dozen buns. Too much. Who eat? I give to neighbour kids."

"Good. And the home worker coming?"

"Yesterday. And today too, later. You know what Ruby like, right? How the weather?"

"Too hot, too humid. But what's new?"

"New therapy working. You miss yesterday. Ruby humming 'Bengawan Solo,' and Papa could sing a few words. He dance some more. Imagine? Those doctors in hospital smart, right?"

"Yeah. And then?"

"You know. The same. When the music stop, he stop too."

We're about to say goodbye when, on impulse, I decide to ask a question I haven't dared ask all these years. "Mum, do you regret moving to Canada?"

A pause before she answers, "All for better, Natalie. I don't like to think about past. Papa not happy living near my family. You know that, right? You not happy. Life there not suit you. Right or not?"

I stare at the blank TV screen. I want to say, *I never wanted to leave*. But I restrain myself and say instead, "You're absolutely right. It turned out better for me, after all. But what a sacrifice for you, leaving your family behind."

"Life is about sacrifice, my daughter."

"Maybe, Mum. Or maybe not."

After we hang up, I sit on top of the bed, trying to still my racing heart. I feel lost. In a city I no longer recognize. Signs of my childhood erased. I can't quite sense the web of continuity that once held me up; I wish I could weave and extend my memories into the present without the clash of regret or turmoil. I feel disoriented, rankled by the harsh absences.

Memories hurt us. Or is it truer to say that it's our refusal to release ourselves from the past that's the cause of our pain?

The storm whips up the trees outside. I watch the violent sway of branches from my seat on the bed. Nature's drama viewed from a safe place, sounds of that outer turmoil muted by the drone of the air conditioning in my room.

I pull out the cloth bag that holds the Oracle booklet and wooden chips. Cup all twelve chips in my hands. What's my question? Drawing a blank. Guess I'm not ready.

Lights off. In the dark, I locate Lung 5, *Chi Ze*, Cubit Marsh, on the radial side of the elbow crease. Press the spot on both arms. This is a water point, a powerful spot on the lung meridian to replenish yin energies and bring down feelings of anxiety.

After treating myself, I fall asleep quickly. In the dream, a mist envelops Mum and me, causing the room to disappear. When the mist clears, the room returns, completely white, stripped of all distraction, suspended instead in a timeless and vast emptiness. In this private enclave, Mum speaks in perfect English, without a trace of Singlish. *Daughter, I appreciate your loyalty. I'm sorry I couldn't save you.*

I jolt awake. Dazed. Slightly aroused, in a disturbing way. I feel ambivalent but reach down to touch myself, thinking of Michelle's body, and how her skin tastes. But my mind keeps flitting back to the young Faridah who lay next to me, teasing me with songs sung close to my ear. Their bodies fuse in my imagination, heat flushing through me until I can't postpone flinging off the sheets any longer.

ten 脈

It was toward the end of Secondary One, only weeks away from the annual school concert.

"Go placidly amid the noise and the haste, and remember what peace there may be in silence."

Miss Rajah was using her left hand to pace us as we recited, as if she was conducting a choir. She cocked her head to one side, to listen to the rhythms of our voices.

I was in the Low Voices. The girls in the High Voices took over once we finished the last line of our section. It amazed me to hear how they twittered and sparkled, their voices bright and light as air, unlike the rumbling timbre of ours in the Low Voices. Then there were the girls in the Chorus. I envied them, because they got to sing those great lines twice around.

After the practice, Faridah and I headed across the street to the vendor outside the corner coffee shop.

"What do you think about the Age of Aquarius?" Faridah asked, gasping from the heat of the *goreng pisang* in her mouth.

"This is the dawning of the Age of Aquarius," I sang rather weakly, unsure of my grasp of the melody.

"Yeah, yeah, yeah . . . *and love will steer the stars* . . . the bloody stars!" Faridah's words were muffled because she was still chewing the sweet deep-fried banana. When she finished eating, she continued, "Those hippies in America! *Hiau* or what? Pretty wild. Love-ins, peace-ins or whatnot, all the sex and drugs. John Lennon and Yoko Ono with their bed-in. What do you think? Shall we do one?"

"When the moon is in the seventh house . . ."

"Hey, don't change the topic."

"I'm not. That's my answer."

"What kind of an answer is that?" She pouted, her hands on her hips.

I shrugged. I didn't like it when she put me on the spot like that. Sometimes it was too much for me. It was impossible to know whether Faridah was joking or serious, since she sometimes uttered rather outrageous things with a solemn expression.

"How can love-ins make a difference? I'm not sure . . ." I sucked on my piece of *pisang*, enjoying the mushy sweetness underneath the crispy batter of tapioca flour.

"Age of Aquarius, man. Supposed to be getting all

peaceful, but where got?" Faridah sounded like a different person whenever she affected Singlish. In slang, she sounded flippant, someone for whom ideas and suggestions could be casually entertained, then dismissed.

"About this po-em . . ." she whispered, spitting the last word into two distinct syllables, ". . . I don't think my father would be happy with 'Desiderata.' Deep down, he's very old-fashioned, even though he likes to show off how sophisticated he is. Best French restaurant for their wedding anniversary, fancy stuff like that. You know, very artsy."

"I thought he was pretty broad-minded."

"Guess so. After all, he was part of *Utusan Melayu* in the early '50s."

"What's that?"

"Chinese people should know Malay history, okay?" She looked exasperatedly at me, but then explained, "Malay newspaper founded in 1939, lasted until 1959. My father wrote a lot for it. He even encouraged parents to send their girls to school. Big deal back then."

"Well then, bet your father won't mind you being part of 'Desiderata.'"

"Maybe. Or maybe too *hiau*. He's forever worrying that Western ideas will corrupt me and my brother. He's already talking about wanting me to get married and give him lots of grandchildren. Gross, huh? Well, maybe not gross . . ." Faridah stared off into the distance, facing Mountbatten Road. I wondered what she was looking at. She continued, "Well, I do want to make my parents happy. Sort of. Except for the lots of children bit. He's always lecturing my brother and me not to get carried away watching those crazy Hollywood movies or BBC programs. Forever emphasizing the importance of traditions."

I thought of Faridah's mother. Aunty Sylvia always looked elegant in her Nonya outfits and accessories: her *baju panjang, sarong kebaya,* all the fancy and ornate pins for her blouses and her hair. She dressed even more Nonya than my own Mah-Mah, who often contented herself with some very Chinese-looking outfits, especially the *samfu.*

"Your father sounds a bit like my Kong-Kong. Scolds my parents—imagine, huh—for allowing me to read MAD and *Beano.* I don't care what the adults say, I need my comics. Weird, grown-ups…"

"Won't be weird when I grow up. I'll be very normal, I'm sure."

I didn't want to stop pursuing my train of thought. "Okay, for example. When he was young, Kong-Kong read lots of European authors, but in translation. These days, he keeps nagging my mother to teach me classical Chinese tales. Ridiculous, right?"

Faridah stared at me, and pursed her lips.

I felt the momentum build. "Then there's my father, who often tells me, *Do what I say and not what I do.* What? Now that's *gila,* okay?"

"Ooh, you're an angry one."

I unclenched my jaw. I wished I knew what I could do to dispel the strong feelings bubbling inside me. I grunted, then walked toward Katong News Agency. What was it I needed to get there? I frowned, trying to recall. Some HB pencils.

Faridah didn't say anything but walked beside me. There was something rather soothing about her following me. It helped me calm down, be less angry.

I stopped in front of the stationery shop, thinking about Faridah's comments about her father. "I don't get it. So your father would mind 'Desiderata'?"

"It's sex, Natalie, that's what my father is worried about."

"Sex? What?"

"He's afraid my brother and I will get into trouble that way, especially me."

"Oh..."

Faridah giggled. "Seriously, when I grow up, I want to make sure I marry a guy that my parents will be proud of."

"Shouldn't you also be happy with your man, huh?"

"Yeah, I guess so. I hope they'll like the one I choose. Nothing worse than parents being disappointed with their children."

I thought seriously about what Faridah was saying. It seemed to me that Papa was already frequently unhappy with me. So what difference could a marriage make? Absolutely nothing. I didn't understand why Faridah was so intent on making her parents happy by marrying. How different we were.

Faridah continued, "So you see . . . 'Desiderata' . . . desired things. That's a very Western idea. I mean, we're not supposed to follow our hearts' desires. We're supposed to stay away from new ideas that take us away from our parents' ways."

My anger returned. I wanted to say that my parents' ways hadn't done too much for me so far. This was a side of Faridah I hadn't seen before. The girl I met on the first day of Secondary One was strong and confident. She knew how to put me in my place and challenge my rudeness.

I blurted out, "Argh, old people, damn it. Superstitious like hell, especially of anything that's new."

"Suspicious. And please don't swear."

"What?"

"Suspicious, not superstitious."

"Okay, okay. So what if I get those two words confused sometimes? I think 'superstitious' also applies." I felt even more cross. How dare she act like she was my teacher? Like she knew better. I fished out my hankie and flicked it vigorously, striking her arm. Then I made some growling sounds and bared my teeth at her.

Inside Katong News Agency, the portable radio was blasting at full volume, a tinny-sounding Tom Jones singing "Pussycat, pussycat, I love you." I paid the Indian shopkeeper for the pencils. I was about to walk off when Faridah stopped me and asked, "Aren't you going to try?"

"Try what?"

"The *tikam*."

"What's the point?"

Ever since seeing the Godzilla movie, I had been trying my luck on the *tikam* board, which tempted me with its depictions of plastic toy prizes. If the ads weren't lying, there was at least one Godzilla somewhere on each board, hidden in one of the white opaque packets. But I didn't feel very hopeful. I'd tried many times before and failed to win it.

"Let me do it." Faridah gave the shopkeeper five cents, then briskly grabbed a packet and yanked it off the board. She pulled at the packet with her teeth, slowly ripping a hole big enough for her thumb and forefinger.

"Hey! How about that!" Godzilla emerged and lay there in her palm. My anger swiftly became a thing of the past. I reached for the tiny creature, but Faridah slipped Godzilla into her pinafore pocket and yanked me out of the shop. We giggled, skipping and racing down Tanjong Katong Road until we paused at Dunman Road, completely winded. We crossed over to the other side, stopping between two large frangipani trees, one with faint pink flowers with orange centres, while the other had intense dark pink blooms. With her hands on my shoulders, Faridah pushed me gently back, until I was up against the trunk of the frangipani tree with the deep pink flowers. I could feel the rough, coarse texture of the bark against my blouse and pinafore. It didn't hurt. It was a pleasant sensation, as if the skin on my back was becoming awakened by that unusual, uneven pressure.

"See? I brought you luck. Takes a special touch to win the prize."

I studied her face, unsure what she was going to do next. She caressed my neck softly with her fingers and whispered, "Okay, this is a good way to start our love-in." She closed her hand around my neck. Her grip was firm, but not so tight that I couldn't breathe.

I pretended to be unperturbed, even though my heart was racing. "What are you doing?"

"Be patient now. I'm testing you."

She pinched open my shirt collar with one hand and then dropped the figure right in. Godzilla landed between my small breasts, nestled in my recently acquired white Maidenform bra. I felt his cold presence and shivered. I fished Godzilla out and smiled down at my new toy.

"Thanks," I said, blushing with gratitude.

"Promise me something."

"What's that?"

"Don't lose it, whatever happens."

"Okay, I promise."

WHEN I got back to Cosmic Pulse, I nodded to Mum, who sat with her left side facing the front of the shop, talking with Kong-Kong as he sliced up ginseng root. I rushed to the back and bolted up the stairs.

In the living room, a group of men were sitting with my father. Everyone dressed in a similar style: the long-sleeved cotton-polyester blend white shirts and black or brown pants. Standard outfit, which Papa wore for work every day. It was the first time Papa had had any of his co-workers over. As medical representatives, they carried briefcases full of pharmaceutical samples, making the rounds of the island's clinics, hospitals and pharmacies. Three of the men lounged in chairs around our small Formica dining table, while the other two sat with my father on the sofa. I recognized Seng Huat, Papa's co-worker who covered Shenton Way area, Chinatown and Rochor, whereas my father covered the Jurong, Bukit Timah and Pasir Panjang areas.

Papa nodded to me and said, "My daughter."

The men either nodded or smiled, but they all shifted uneasily, as if I had caught them in the middle of something illicit.

"Go placidly amid the noise," I mumbled as I disappeared into my room.

Usually, when my parents had visitors, I would close my door tightly, not wanting to be disturbed by the sound of chatter, but this time I kept a slight gap between my door and the frame. I wondered if there was something important afoot, and I didn't want to miss it.

"Can't be true. Just stupid rumour maybe spread by our competitor." The voice was wheezy. Possibly a long-time smoker.

"All my years at the company, I never hear this before. How can?" My father's voice sounded even tighter than usual. I could picture the muscles in his neck bulging, how he would get before one of his nasty moods.

Other voices piped up, almost all talking at the same time.

"*Si tiu.*"

"Filthy buggers."

"*Chee buy*, son of a dirty *kah chern.*"

I winced at the sounds of the Hokkien swear words.

One of them had a youngish voice whose timbre might have landed him in the High Voices if he were in our "Desiderata" group.

"Company going to break our balls, I think."

I cringed even more. Crude language sounded extra-sinister coming from a wheezy set of lungs.

"Not so loud," warned my father.

The telephone rang. A few moments after my father picked it up, I heard him shouting for me to pick up the call. I opened the door and glanced coolly at the men before I took the call. They continued to talk loudly as if I wasn't even there.

It was Faridah. I felt my heart lurch with excitement at her suggestion.

"Okay, I'll go ask," I said before I hung up the phone.

I went downstairs in search of Mum. The shop was momentarily empty of customers. I found Mum sitting behind the counter, reading yet another Chinese novel. I tapped her elbow cautiously. She looked up, still in a daze.

"Can Faridah stay over tomorrow night? We want to rehearse 'Desiderata' together."

"We going church next day."

"She can come, right?"

"What about her parents? They mind or not?"

"She said they're fine with it. They're very *modern*," I said, careful to emphasize that last word.

"Papa finished meeting yet?"

"No. What is it about, Mum?"

"Company business. Nothing for you to worry about."

THE next day, I followed Mum to the market.

It was past eight. The market was crowded. We made our way to the meat and produce sections first. Mum bought mackerels and *kangkong* spinach and asked the Indian spice seller to make up a fresh batch of *rempah* mix to stuff the fish with. Then shallots, garlic, fresh galangal, red chilies and ginger. A handful of calamansi limes.

Finally we made our way to the section of the market that consisted of stalls selling cooked foods and hot and cold beverages.

"What you want for breakfast?"

"*Putu mayam*," I replied without hesitation, then continued, "Hot *tau chui*."

After ordering a glass of hot soy milk for me, Mum told me to sit at a free table while she went to order the *putu mayam*.

I removed the rubber band and unwrapped the packet as soon as Mum returned. The outside of the packet was the usual day-old *Straits Times* newspaper. I glanced at it quickly. "Wife Runs Amok and Kills Husband with Cleaver." Inside was a smooth, dark green banana leaf wrapped around the steaming hot food. I loved the contrast of textures: the cooked string hoppers, so much like our Chinese rice vermicelli, except slightly thicker and wound around like nests. To one side of the *putu mayam* were scoops of golden brown sugar and freshly grated coconut.

"Want some?" I asked Mum, noticing that she hadn't bought enough for two of us.

She pulled out a smaller packet wrapped like a pyramid, with a slight gap at the top. I peered in.

"*Nasi lemak!*" I stuck my nose into the gap and inhaled appreciatively.

"Don't be greedy. Eat your own."

Mum ordered *kopi-O*, her favourite dark coffee sweetened with sugar. We focused on eating and said nothing to one another until we were both finished.

"Think your friend like my stuffed fish?"

"For tonight, you mean?"

She nodded, deep in thought, but not saying more.

"Sure, why not?"

"I make extra-hot."

"Okay." I shrugged my shoulders. "Can we go now?"

AT 5:30 that evening, the doorbell downstairs rang.

"I'll go."

"No, I go. You don't know how open that front metal gate," retorted Mum.

"Who's that?" asked Papa.

"A friend of Natalie's come stay over." Mum started to head downstairs.

"Oh?"

Faridah came up the stairs dressed in a white kurta top, blue Lee jeans and a pair of blood red Puma suede sneakers.

"Wow, groovy," I whistled.

She smiled and greeted my parents. Papa was listening to his record of George Beverly Shea singing hymns on the headphones. He gave a quick nod to Faridah and went back to his music.

IT TURNED out that Faridah loved the mackerel stuffed with *rempah*, and the *kangkong* fried with dried shrimp and sambal. Mum had even made some coconut rice, inspired by her morning meal of *nasi lemak*.

"Finger-licking *bagus!*" Faridah exclaimed, giving a local twist to Colonel Saunders. She licked her right index finger and made a number one sign.

All of us laughed, even Papa. I looked at my parents, stunned that Faridah's presence somehow brought momentary cheer to my home. I felt tender pangs in my chest more than once as I ate.

The house settled into a hush after dinner. Mum washed dishes in the small sink at the back, and Papa returned to his hymns.

Faridah and I went into my room and took out the practice sheets for "Desiderata."

"I like that we end on that low, descending tone when we get to the word 'silence.' You know what I mean?" She was staring down at the paper, very focused.

"Do you snore?" I asked Faridah.

She laughed and poked me in the ribs. "There you go, being rude again."

"I can't stand snoring. My father snores. Sometimes you can hear him in the living room."

"Don't your parents sleep together in the same bed?"

"Mostly not. Papa falls asleep on the sofa with the TV on. Mum wakes up later to switch it off around 1:00 a.m."

"Huh! No sex please, we're not British?"

I stuck out my tongue at my witty friend.

"You know your parents' late-night habits? Must mean you're awake too."

I looked away, overcome with shame. There was no way I could tell her the truth. I couldn't fall asleep until he did. I kept quiet and looked down at my copy of "Desiderata." Desired things. What I wanted right then was to run away with Faridah, leave this miserable predicament in my home and spend my life with her.

"I like 'Desiderata' a lot. Wish I could be in the chorus,

singing."

"Come on, let's sing it together now." She placed her hand gently on mine.

It took a few seconds to agree on the key before we launched softly into *"You are a child of the universe no less than the trees and the stars; you have a right to be here."*

"Let's sing it a few more times," I requested.

By the tenth time, Faridah was looking at me with a puzzled look on her face. "What's the matter?"

"What do you mean?"

"You're crying."

"I just—I don't know how to describe this feeling."

I'd never sung like that before. The only other times I sang were in the congregation at church. To sing in a quiet, reflective way, sitting side by side on the bed with my best friend, hearing myself sound out those lyrics, made me feel—if only for those moments—that I was loved by some divine force in the universe, some vast, mysterious entity, unconditional in its acceptance of me. Was that God? I didn't have a name for it.

"Natalie, you're so strange. Doesn't matter. Maybe that's why I like you." She leaned toward me and lightly touched my lips with hers, barely grazing them before she pulled away.

"What . . . ?"

"Silly, don't you know about kissing?"

"No one's ever kissed me before."

"Let me show you again," she said, and proceeded to kiss me, this time with much more confidence. Her lips pressed firmly against mine.

This led me to cry even more, but it didn't stop me from kissing her back. I liked feeling the warmth travel down my back, right down to my toes. It was the same kind of feeling I got when I read a book I liked or when I heard a song on the radio that moved me. Something else was happening too, a heat rising up between my legs. The heat was familiar, yet felt different. I liked it this time, because I felt close to Faridah. Papa never kissed me. He always had his eyes closed. And I would pretend I was asleep. But I could feel the sticky sensation of his erection when he placed my hands on it. I would sneak a look at it sometimes, rising like a snake between his thighs.

Faridah kissing me was very different, I decided.

"You know what I'm glad about?" Faridah said, as she drew slightly away from me, gazing into my eyes.

"What?"

"That we're both girls."

"Why?"

"We get to be in the same class in a girls' school, and now we can be this close."

"Do other girls kiss like this?"

"In America they do. Free love, remember?"

"So this is free love? Not bad."

Faridah switched off the light and pulled me down beside her. "Do you ever get lonely?" she whispered into my ear as she stroked my arm.

"I feel lonely all the time," I confessed easily. No one had asked me this question before.

"I want you to run to me whenever you're lonely. You won't forget me, will you? No matter what happens to us?"

"I'll never forget you," I said.

eleven 脈

Run to me whenever you're lonely.

The Bee Gees tune comes to mind moments before the alarm clock blares out. I slam my hand down on the Stop button crossly. The song keeps playing in my head. Faridah had said that, the first time we kissed.

I've been thinking of her over the weekend, while doing some sightseeing. I acted like a foreigner and joined a group tour to Jurong Bird Park on Saturday. Last night, anticipating our meeting today, I didn't do much, but kept going over in my mind how I felt seeing her on Friday night.

From down the hallway come thuds of luggage against walls and half-opened doors as guests drag themselves and their belongings toward the elevator.

Half an hour later, at the Tin Heang coffee shop across the street, I order a bowl of Teochew porridge, along with fried smelt and a dish of mustard greens. It's 1:00 p.m., my first meal of the day. The *kopi tiam* is bustling. I'm surrounded by the lunch crowd eating at tables or ordering takeout.

After finishing lunch, I walk toward Marine Parade Housing Estate. While waiting for the pedestrian light to turn green at the corner of Joo Chiat and Marine Parade roads, I spot Faridah across the street, sitting on the front steps of the library.

On this side of the road is a stretch of old trees. This is where the shoreline used to be. That beach has disappeared, replaced by the main thoroughfare that defines the outer boundary of the housing estate—Housing and Development Board flats built by the government in the early 1970s. The HDB estate was first of its kind built on reclaimed land, part of the vast and ambitious east coast land reclamation project started in the 1960s.

After crossing the road, I wave at Faridah to catch her attention. "Hey, there." I smile as I approach her.

We take the nearest underpass to the beach. Above the tunnel is the East Coast Parkway, the rush of traffic reaching us as a low, muffled drone. The walls of the underpass are pristine, except for a single line of graffiti: *Fuck police*. We encounter a handful of people using the underpass, mostly elderly folks. As it's a Monday, most people are at work or in school. We spot a few *ang mos*, either expatriates or tourists. We head toward the ocean, saying little. It's as if the silence from Friday night is still stubbornly clinging to us.

Hardly a trace of wind. The air is slathered with humidity. I sense that extra layer of pressure wrap itself around me. As we stroll along the pedestrian path heading east, I notice a jagged line of cargo ships on the far horizon.

"How much longer are you off?"

"My boss has been kind. He said I could take another two weeks off, as long as I return ready and able to function at my previous level of efficiency. Think I'll go back after the memorial service." She pauses, looking disturbed. "I'm not used to time off. I like being busy. A PR person is always on the go. I thrive best when challenged. Worse to be at home, with nothing to do except think of Selim all day."

"How horrible."

"It's the hardest thing I've ever faced . . ."

Two girls and their parents race past us on rollerblades, squealing in delight. Once on the sand, we take our sandals off and continue walking. We never went to the beach together when we were young. But that was an entirely different beach, anyway. The shoreline was back where Marine Parade Road now is. I don't know for sure, but I would guess the shoreline is now about one and a half miles farther out.

I like the sensation of walking barefoot on the sand. My feet feel relaxed by the soft and giving warmth. I take a deep breath and decide to be direct. "I'm not sure how I can help you, Faridah."

"Selim insisted I ask you for forgiveness. Isn't it too late?" Her eyes redden with tears.

"Maybe not. Maybe what he said has something useful to offer us."

She stops and stares at me, her eyes flaring with a fierce energy. "You hardly knew him. But you trust that he was wise?"

I close my eyes for a few seconds. *Yes, I knew him.*

Faridah continues, "There are quite a few things I want to tell you. Just not sure where to start."

We walk to a log near the water's edge. There's no one within earshot, only occasional strollers, preoccupied with their own thoughts and conversations. We look out at the breakwater. I allow my gaze to drift past the artificial barrier of rocks and toward the hazy horizon.

"The police have closed the case, concluding there's no evidence of foul play."

"Yeah? That's fast. What about that strange clue, if we can call it a clue."

"What's that?" She looks blankly at me.

"Godzilla's touch. What he said to you, what he wrote on the piece of paper he left on the bed."

"Oh, yes. That's true," she answers flatly, casting her eyes down.

I'm surprised at her tone. She seems quite uncomfortable about the note. It reminds me of the first time we spoke about Selim on the phone; it seemed then that she had a similar need to avoid this issue.

"The day after the suicide, Adam and I had to go look at him at the coroner's. His face was . . . dark purple. A darker line across his neck, where . . . where . . ." She pauses, looking pale. "They had sliced open his skull. There was a line just above his eyebrows where the autopsy cut was, but the coroner had placed the top half back on, and sewn up the scalp. His body . . . oh god . . . there were rope marks all over his body. It was dreadful." Her voice quivers. Gasping, almost out of breath. She bites into her lower lip. "The officer in charge of the investigation said that the autopsy ruled out any kind of drug poisoning or subcranial trauma, or things such as stroke or blockage. He also said the rope marks suggested he was into some kind of bondage, but that would have been consensual. At least, not the cause of death."

"He was so casual about the bondage?"

"Yeah, shocking, I know. As if he saw this kind of thing a lot. He sounded dismissive. Which is odd, considering he was one of their own. I tried to argue with him. Right there, in the morgue. Standing over Selim's body. I was shivering. From rage, from shock. Both. But Adam just stood beside me, completely mute. It was awful. I felt as if they were ganging up on me, looking at me as if, as if . . ." She pauses at this point, and her jaw muscles clench. ". . . I were a hysterical woman."

"Fucking disgusting."

Faridah startles from hearing me swear, straightening up. "If Selim were the officer in charge of such an investigation . . . I know him, he wouldn't have pooh-poohed such a detail."

"I'm sure. He seemed very dedicated to his work."

"But bondage? I had no idea. What else don't I know? It's . . . it's so wrong, not to know. He was my son, after all."

Her tone suggests disbelief, as if she were talking about a stranger whose identity she can't quite accept.

"You must think I've gone mad. I feel responsible, because I told him about what your father did. He kept asking me to repeat the story. He had an excessive fascination with it. Is this my imagination? I mean, how could it be a coincidence?"

I shake my head and look at her helplessly, not knowing what to say.

"I can't help but think that Selim's preoccupation with your story must have something to do with his death. It's just that . . . it doesn't make any logical sense. I don't get the connection." She frowns, a look of consternation on her face.

After a long pause, she asks, her expression almost pleading, "What do you make of it?"

"Not sure." I feel dumbfounded. There's something I'm grappling with. Something to do with what we were talking about a little earlier. The thought is unclear, still hazy, but I must try to give voice to it, to what's rising up inside me. I watch the waves ebb and flow, slowly creeping up the sand, closer to our feet.

"I suspect you had your own reasons to tell him. About me, what my father did. I mean, not just so he could feel better."

"What do you mean?"

"I'm saying . . . maybe you couldn't get over it. It left a mark on you." I shiver, hearing what I've just said. That word, "mark," as if I've discovered a wound that had been previously invisible.

"I blamed myself for what happened to you. Being with you was what made your father so angry. How could we have continued?" She chokes up.

I think, *How crazy to blame yourself*. But hadn't I blamed her for my own misery when she left me? I swallow hard before I try to say more.

"You carried that guilt with you. A terrible burden. Felt you had to say something to your son, who was also experiencing being hurt by his father. Like I had been." A long, chilling tremor grips my body. I feel a little crazy, unable to stop my body from shaking. No, it's the opposite of crazy. It's a kind of knowing, that reaches further. Closer to the core of truth.

"What are you saying?" Her eyes flare up. "You're agreeing with me, that I'm to blame?"

"No! Not that. I'm saying . . ." I gasp at the realization that surfaces. ". . . you felt deeply for him in his suffering. And in feeling for him, you must have been remembering what it was like for me."

Faridah reaches out and grips my arm. "I could never forget."

I sigh and look at one of the ships on the far horizon. Her eyes follow my gaze. We've left so much unsaid. She has never said anything to me all these years about what she witnessed that day.

I don't know how I managed to survive the turmoil at the end of Secondary Four that year, how I managed to do my O levels. Faridah avoided me, wouldn't talk to me. She looked ghastly every time I saw her in class. It was a year of hell.

Faridah got married just over two years after our breakup. That would have been early 1978, soon after pre-university. It all happened so fast. It was difficult for me to hear the gossip. Then I got an invitation to the wedding. It stung me to read the details printed on the inside of the card, without even a personal note from Faridah. I declined, given that Kong-Kong had passed away only a few months before.

I suspect that Faridah might not have married Adam so soon after school, and might have proceeded directly to university, if she hadn't gotten pregnant. In those days, it was quite the taboo to have sex before marriage, and a worse taboo to get pregnant out of wedlock. She and Adam had no choice but to get married quickly. What a dreadful irony, then, that she miscarried that first time, soon after the wedding. It was a loss that no one could acknowledge. Not publicly, at least.

At that time, it had seemed to me that my friendship with Faridah was over. A few months before I left Singapore, I half-heartedly sent her a card with my forwarding address in Canada, not expecting to hear back from her. But she wrote back. Only three terse lines on a scrap of paper ripped along the top edge, accompanied by that tiny Godzilla in a plain letter-sized envelope. I carried that envelope inside my jacket when I stepped onto the plane with my parents.

I clung to that precious toy monster and those few lines on that piece of paper, because that was all I had: *Ps. You left this in my pencil case. Please don't lose this again, okay? And don't forget me, please.*

I'm roused from my memories by a voice calling out, *"Nasi, nasi . . . nasi lemak!"*

A lanky boy hurries up to us, offering us packets of *nasi lemak* from a large plastic basket. Faridah buys two packets, but frowns worriedly at him. "Careful, you could get caught, yeah?"

We unwrap the packets: yesterday's *Straits Times* on the outside with a banana leaf inside, and the rice, warm and fragrant still, the fried *ikan bilis* anchovies and rectangle of fried egg nudged against a generous scoop of sambal. We lift the plastic spoons and dig in.

The wind has picked up. The smell of the ocean drifts up to us as we eat.

I cast my mind back to our last comments before we fell silent.

"For years . . . all this time . . . I've held onto blame too. Except mine was directed at my father. For what he did. On one level, if I simply listened to that angry young woman in me right now, I'd say to you, if we're looking to blame anyone, we should point the finger at my father, the one who did those horrendous things." I feel the flush of heat travel up my neck to my ears and cheeks. "But I can't be that locked up in hatred. Can't afford to . . ."

". . . stay tied up . . ."

"Be possessed by the past."

The gulls swoop down onto the small mound of sea-weed washed up to the left of us. They seem to have found some food, perhaps a dead fish. I lift a finger to the edge of Faridah's mouth to wipe off a stray grain of rice. To my surprise, she doesn't flinch away.

My mind drifts back to that party two years ago. The last time I saw Faridah. The party was on a stretch of beach east of where we're sitting now. I recall Philip sitting there, looking so uncomfortable.

"What about Philip?"

"What about him?" She answers quickly, frowning at me.

"Did the police question him?"

"Yes." She averts her eyes while she continues eating. "Philip is devastated."

Devastated. I echo that word in my mind, repeating it a few times.

"I need to accept that Selim hid things from me. We cling to the necessity of secrets. For the sake of survival."

She sounds uncannily like Selim. The Selim I spoke to at Harry's Bar, all philosophical yet obviously vulnerable.

"He must have thought it was important to have some things hidden," I say, following her line of thinking.

"Isn't that the problem—we've learned too well that there's a reason to be guarded?"

"We all have reasons to fear, especially to fear betrayal." I don't know why I say that. The words come out of me, without my complete understanding, and yet it feels right.

"Fear betrayal..." she repeats, mulling over this notion. "Betrayal, abandonment, rejection."

A shudder passes through me. I felt utterly betrayed and abandoned when Faridah stopped seeing me.

"I knew Selim was gay," she proclaims.

"So that wasn't a secret."

"No."

"Was that why you told him about us having been lovers?"

"Yes. It was my way of telling him I understood. That I accepted him. I told him I regretted that circumstances didn't allow me to continue to be with you. But I could at least support his choices, whomever he chose to love, to be close to."

"What about Adam?"

"He must have known...but he couldn't handle talking about it. Selim and I both understood—implicitly— that it was too charged for Adam. That's why we never brought it up in front of him."

Faridah breaks down, sobbing. She crosses her arms over her chest, and bends forward slightly. "If only I hadn't told him that story about you."

"You mustn't blame yourself. You must stop."

I bury my toes deeper in the sand. I feel an urge to do something to break out of this constraint I feel inside. I use a twig to draw in the sand. Trigraph 53, Assistance of the Spirits, expressing a wish for extraordinary help. Four characters for Heaven on the top line, two Humans in the middle line, and one Earth on the bottom line. Trigraph 53 predicts the end of obstruction. I guess I'm hoping that something will shift in Faridah and she can stop blaming herself.

Faridah continues to cry, her sobs getting louder. I move closer and put my arms around her. When she finally stops weeping, she wipes the tears away with a small batik hankie emblazoned with a bright orange butterfly. Its wings collapse and tremble in her clutch.

In a calmer voice, she says, "You haven't told me much about your life in Toronto, but I've noticed how much you've changed over the years. You're not the sad young woman who left Singapore in '79. And you deserve . . ." Her voice breaks off.

I want to say, *So do you*. Instead, I say, *"Go placidly amid the noise and the haste, and remember what peace there may be in silence."* The ocean rushes into my voice, echoing the sounds of the words.

"Especially do not feign affection. Neither be cynical about

love . . ." Faridah responds, reciting lines from the poem.

"You remember."

A bright flicker returns to her eyes. She smiles warmly at me. "I loved being so carefree."

The ocean by this time has crept farther inland, now almost touching our bare feet. We get up without needing to prompt each other and head back toward the old Katong we know.

THE rain starts off light and fast, angling against our bodies. Faridah and I run for shelter, making it back to the underpass just as the downpour begins. The echoing sound of rain surrounds us as we walk underneath the roar of the East Coast Parkway and through to the other side. When we emerge from the cavernous passage into the open, the rain has become heavier, more insistent.

We dart from one block of flats to the next, quickly becoming drenched. The air vibrates with the sounds of many windows being closed, a clamorous chorus of withdrawal. The rain is relentless, creating even greater ruckus than the banging shut of windows.

We hail a taxi. Faridah gives the driver her address. I shiver as the rain evaporates off my skin in the air-conditioned car. When we arrive and step out of the taxi, the air is still charged with humidity, despite the storm. My body is shocked by the sudden transition from air conditioning back to tropical heat.

The sound of her key in the lock, then the brief clunk as Faridah pushes the metal gates to the edges of the doorframe, open me up to memories of this once-familiar ritual. I haven't been here since 1975. The stairs up to her flat feel narrower. Of course, I was smaller then.

I feel disoriented by the altered atmosphere inside. I still connect this flat with the time when it was only Faridah and her parents who lived here. Her older brother had already moved to Jakarta by the time I met her. I knew these rooms well, knew the people in that family and liked being here. Entering the living room, I half-expect to see Aunty Sylvia, greeting me with her warm eyes and that sparkle of a welcoming voice. To glimpse Uncle Osman quietly reading and mumbling under his breath on the balcony, while steadily fanning his face. They're gone, leaving one after the other, in early 2006, he lasting only five months after her death. But they weren't even living here when that happened. I don't know where they had moved to.

Faridah has suffered three major losses in less than two years. But this is surely the most unbearable—losing her son to suicide.

"I never realized just how lonely it felt here until these past few weeks, when I've been the only one home during the day," Faridah proclaims, as if picking up the tenor of my thoughts.

I gaze in the direction of the balcony. A cage hangs suspended from the ceiling. The compact, bright yellow body of a canary startles me with its quick movements. I walk up to the cage to get a closer look.

"It was my father's, then Selim inherited it."

The rain pelts against the open windows, splashing into the flat. Faridah rushes to close them. I follow her back to the kitchen, where she's retrieving two bamboo poles that were perched in their outside slots below the windows. Both poles of laundry are now dripping wet. Using a double-pronged stick, she raises each pole to rest on brackets just below the ceiling.

"Damn," she mutters, oblivious to my presence for a few moments before she remembers to offer me a clean towel to dry myself off.

I return to the living room, surveying the decor. It must have been crowded in this three-bedroom flat when the children were young. Three generations in three rooms. Aunty Sylvia and Uncle Osman lived here with Faridah and Adam until Selim was ten and Christina three.

I heard that Faridah and Adam moved in right after they married. Quite the anomaly, since it's usually the wife who lives with her husband's parents. Apparently, Adam's parents wouldn't welcome her into their house; they blamed her for getting pregnant. Implied she did it to trap Adam. They had hoped he would further his studies overseas, perhaps enter medical school. Instead, because of Faridah's pregnancy, he opted to marry and enter teacher's college in Singapore. I'm guessing he didn't want to take too long before getting a stable, well-paid job. He seems to have enjoyed teaching. Look where it got him: vice-principal of a secondary school for almost eight years now.

The living-room walls are a peaceful sage green, but they were once a cheerful yellow. I loved the vibrancy of this room when I was young, such a contrast to the cool, dark interior of our rooms above Cosmic Pulse.

Darkness, brightness, the range of colours, even the feel of space around me: I had been very impressionable, easily overwhelmed by external forces. Vulnerable.

I sit down on the tan leather sofa, next to the hexagonal Moroccan brass table. I remember this side table, which used to display Uncle Osman's collection of miniature teak elephants he had collected in his travels throughout Asia. Before he started working for *Utusan Melayu* and, later, *The Straits Times*.

I look out, past the sliding doors to the view outside. The rain seems not to be letting up, forming a thick curtain outside the balcony. The bird, however, seems unfazed by the weather, continuing to chirp occasionally.

Faridah enters the living room with a tray bearing two cups of black tea and a plate of almond cookies. She seems uneasy, unsure where she wants to sit. Finally, she positions herself on the armchair across from me and, after some fidgeting, leans forward, cradling the cup of tea in both hands. But without saying anything.

"I'll leave as soon as the rain stops. Or I could hail a taxi after drinking this tea?" I look questioningly at her.

"Why don't you stay for dinner? They'll be home in a couple of hours anyway."

I STAND at the entrance to Selim's room while drying my hair with the towel. He's not here, but everything in this room still bears witness to his presence: the clothes that hang in the half-open closet, books and CDs neatly arranged on shelves. A shiver runs down my back. I'm afraid. Afraid of a room that's filled with his absence. I close my eyes. He died here. Committed the ultimate surrender behind closed doors, to loud music. While his family was elsewhere in the flat, unsuspecting. Is this why it's deeply unsettling?

Benkulen Bound. I form the words in my mind without saying them. *Why did you do it?* The tremor returns.

Faridah joins me in the doorway, looking into the shadowy emptiness. "I have gone in there countless times since his death, but it doesn't seem to get any easier."

To my left, the computer sits on his desk, the screen black. I hesitantly move toward it. The windows thud above the desk as the wind continues to howl outside.

"The police looked through everything, including files on the computer, but they didn't find anything suspicious," Faridah offers.

They couldn't have found Selim's cellphone. They'd have contacted me a long time ago if they had read those text messages.

Across from the desk, on the other wall, stands a low bookcase with a mix of books: on the top shelf, *Romeo and Juliet* and *King Lear*, a few novels by Edmund White and James Baldwin, a collection of stories by Alfian Sa'at and a couple of detective novels. There's also a small, tattered book with black masking tape down the spine, marked with white ink: *The First Book of Codes*.

India ink. Its unmistakeable look. That's what was used a lot from the 1950s until the late 1970s. I lift the book out and notice that the full title inside the front cover has the additional phrase *"and Ciphers."* A stamp proclaims the book's prior ownership. A school in Michigan. Date of publication: 1956. In the table of contents, the first heading is "Keeping Secrets," followed by "Your First Code" and then "Codes and Ciphers."

The bottom shelf is entirely filled with philosophy books: Kant, Spinoza, Schopenhauer and a lot of Nietzsche, one with a title that is rather intriguing: *The Gay Science*. The title in German, *Die Frohliche Wissenschaft*.

I pull the book off the shelf and flip through it. A scribbled *Yes!* on the sticky note next to the meaning of "gay": joyful and light-hearted, a lack of solemnity. *Gai Saber*, the art of song cultivated by medieval troubadours of Provence. I notice more small yellow sticky notes in sections. Interesting, to read that the *Wissenschaft* Nietzsche had in mind conveys a gravity-defying spirit evoked by the songs of troubadours celebrating their loves.

I close the book. "Can I borrow this?"

"Of course."

I scan the clear plastic container of anime DVDs.

"Selim was interested in anime?"

"He watched those ones all the time and occasionally borrowed from the library, but I think he sometimes sent away for them."

"What's this one about?" I randomly pick one out: *Voices of a Distant Star.*

"No idea. You know . . ." She pauses, and tucks her hands into her pockets. ". . . other than the police and the family, you're the first person who's stepped into his room."

"I understand. Even I find it hard to be near his things."

She comes close enough to touch my shoulder with the tips of her fingers, very gently and tentatively. Slowly turns to face me. "You're finally here . . . How you've changed, Nat. Even from the last time I saw you."

"I've felt quite different in the past couple of years. I suppose that's inevitable," I reply, thinking of Papa's stroke.

"Yes, it must be rough. Your father—"

"He . . ." I feel on the verge of telling her everything. About how my father abused me all those years. From the time I was not quite six to just before that awful incident in '75. But I mustn't tell her. Not now, when she is so overcome with grief. Maybe not ever.

She continues, "Middle age is weird. I find myself feeling a lot of regret. Sometimes I feel as if I'm still that teenager. The way I'm living these days doesn't quite suit me. I wonder, how would I change my life if I could?"

"What do you mean?"

"I can't talk about it right now." She shakes her head vigorously. Her eyes mist up, though her tears are held in check. "I...I...I'm truly sorry, Natalie." Her hands grasp mine firmly. "I thought it was more important to marry and have a family. What an irony that I chose someone my father didn't completely approve of."

Irony indeed. I wince to hear her words. We chose different paths, and for years, I have felt this vast and unbridgeable rift between us. But here, in this moment, I feel an opening in me. I suppose it's a kind of acceptance.

I lean forward and wrap my arms around her. She receives the hug, and holds me without hesitation.

"Good thing we didn't go the same way as Romeo and Juliet, huh?"

She lets go and looks askance at me. "As weird as ever."

I smile tenderly at her. The desire is there, in my depths. A pulse that has refused to disappear.

"Look," I say, nodding in the direction of the window above Selim's computer. The torrent of rain has stopped. Sunlight streams through the window grill, creating a tiny pattern of light and shadow on the desk. I'm suddenly aware of a heavy fatigue. My legs ache; my eyes can barely stay open.

"Feeling drowsy. Must be jet lag."

"You could take a nap if you want." She nods in the direction of Selim's bed.

"I . . . I'm not sure . . ." I stammer nervously.

She looks pained. Her eyes widen, while her mouth opens an almost imperceptible amount, as if to swallow a small gulp of air. The moment passes quickly.

"Or the sofa in the living room. Can't offer Christina's bed, because she's so fussy about us even entering her room when she's not here. Take your pick."

I nod. "Okay. It will be quieter in here."

"I'll call you when dinner's ready if you haven't woken up by then."

After she leaves the room, I wander back to the CD player and push the Play button. A cut from a Saint Germain CD comes on. How surprising. Having been inundated with pop music in the malls and restaurants, this is such a contrast. New Jazz, the last thing I expected. The repetitive, trance-like chant runs like an undercurrent, supporting the fluid nuances of improvisation. It reminds me of Kinbaku—structure supplemented with subtle variation. Leaving the music on, I drift toward the bed and cautiously sit down, wondering if the sheet and pillowcases still bear some trace of his scent. Finally, too tired to resist, I lie down and close my eyes.

NOTHING seems out of the ordinary at first. I have a sense that it's daytime somewhere beyond this corridor. Sounds of happy chattering filter through to me from the room ahead. I make out the shadowy outline and a hint of light leaking through the gap under the door.

As I walk toward the sound, my hand runs along the wall, smooth as skin, yet so icy cold that I shiver down to my toes. The wall changes, forming rough bumps as I move my hand along the length of it.

A wave of dread passes through me. I want to enter the room, to talk to the people inside, yet I'm terrified of what I will find. I put my ear to the door and listen. I recognize the voice of the canary. Something ominous about its singing. I try to speak, but no sounds emerge from my throat.

I am roused by the rattling of metal gates, followed by a door creaking open. My body feels chilled.

Adam's voice drifts into my sleep-drugged state. I sit up, shaken by the odd dream. Selim's room is silent. The canary's voice has disappeared. My body feels sluggish, as if water-logged. My mind flashes back to those early days in Toronto when I had the recurring nightmares. What is it about nightmares that's so paradoxical? They leave me feeling extremely drained, yet agitated at the same time.

I STUMBLE out to find Adam relaxing in the leather armchair, legs up on the ottoman. He holds a glass of Bacardi and Coke in both hands. He glances up at me and nods. He looks tired, with pronounced shadows under his eyes.

"How was your flight?"

"Always seems too long." I don't want to say it, but the words rush through my mind, *Worsened by the circumstances*.

"Kind of boring, right?" He attempts a smile, but I can see that he's preoccupied.

I notice grey in his sideburns. He looks gaunt from the strain. Even so, Adam is a good-looking man, broad-shouldered and tall. He's tanned, with noticeable fine wrinkles around his eyes.

"Christina's picking up some *kueh*," he calls to Faridah, who doesn't bother to come out from the kitchen. This seems not to faze him. He continues to slowly sip his drink, looking dull-eyed. He turns on the TV. Ten minutes later, Christina arrives home, looking rather dishevelled in her ACJC school uniform.

"Hello, Aunty Natalie," she greets me in a monotone and rushes into her room.

Soon enough, she's back in the living room and joins me on the sofa as we continue to watch the news on SBC, the English channel. When it ends, Christina jumps up and goes into the kitchen to help her mother.

At dinner, we gather at the round table under a lamp that casts a muted orb of light on the black veneer surface. Faridah and Christina bring out plates of food: deep-fried *garoupa* fish topped with fresh chilies and sprigs of fresh coriander, wedges of lime rimming the circumference of the plate; water convolvulus fried with sambal; a plate of steamed prawns, shells on. After the plates of rice are brought out and everyone is seated, Adam fixes an intense gaze on me before carefully placing the palms of his hands together, his slender fingertips pointing up as he closes his eyes. Faridah and Christina follow suit, but I keep my eyes open as Adam says grace. His lower lip protrudes, yet he barely moves his mouth as he mumbles. "Dear Heavenly Father, we give thanks that You've brought our beloved sister Natalie safely back to Singapore. Bless this meal and bless everyone at the table. Amen."

Faridah and Christina have barely opened their eyes when Adam turns to me. "What's it like living in Canada?"

"In what way?"

"I hear it's rather liberal."

"I guess you could say that, relative to Singapore."

Adam raises his eyebrows. I don't know if he's appalled at my direct answer, or if he's impressed.

"We read that the country now allows marriage for homosexuals."

"Uh-huh . . ."

"That's pushing it, don't you think? I mean, we need to be tolerant, but . . ."

"Adam, please . . ." Faridah looks pleadingly at him.

"My father is looking for a reason not to send me to North America for uni." Christina flashes me a pleading look, then casts her eyes down at her food.

"I don't want my daughter to become corrupted by those kinds of values. She's . . . all we have left now." His eyes redden, and he chews his food with great difficulty.

"I beg to differ. Loving someone of the same sex isn't merely a Western phenomenon. And it's not a problem." I stare at Adam disbelievingly. How could I have thought that, just because he is an educator, he wasn't homophobic? Heat rises behind my ears and travels up to my temples. "I guess you'll have to trust that Christina will find the best way for herself. Besides, she doesn't look like a dyke to me." I wink cheekily at Christina.

"Aunty Natalie, you're so-oo funny."

"Glad you appreciate my sense of humour."

"Look, I'm serious. I don't want my daughter to get into the wrong crowd." Adam taps his fingers on the table between us, trying to drawn my attention back to him.

"Don't mind him," Faridah interjects. "He's still in his school administrator role." She places her hand firmly on top of his. I'm not sure if it's a gesture of affection or an attempt to restrain him.

Toward the end of dinner, Adam says, "It's very kind of you to come all the way here to support my wife. You must know it means a lot to her." He blinks, and a tear escapes down his left cheek. "But whom can I talk to? What do I tell my colleagues at school? As vice-principal, I have to be so careful what comes out of my mouth. It would be devastating if word got out that my son killed himself."

"So, you didn't say anything about the circumstances of ..."

"People have been good about not asking awkward questions."

"Christina, go wash the dishes," Faridah insists.

The young woman looks forlorn, but dutifully clears the table. When she's out of the room, Adam says, "We published an obituary in *The Straits Times*."

"It only said 'sudden and unexpected death.'" Faridah adds.

We sit there in silence for a few minutes, until Adam offers to drive me back to the hotel. I decline. "It's not far to walk. The exercise will do me good."

"Are you sure?"

I nod and get up to leave.

"I'll talk to you tomorrow," I promise Faridah as she walks me downstairs. She smiles and pulls the metal gates together between us.

I walk back to the hotel along a different route, turning left and going down to the end of the block of flats, the shops all closed at this time of night. The light from the sky hasn't completely disappeared, but the overhead lamps beam down like reassuring guardians. Across the street stands a signboard advertising a Shaolin White Crane martial arts school. I make a left at Joo Chiat Road and head for the hotel.

At Joo Chiat and Tembeling, a *kopi tiam* is buzzing with customers. There are three food stalls inside: one selling wonton *mee*, another barbecued pork and Hainanese chicken on rice, and a Malay stall offering *nasi padang*. From the back of the coffee shop, the radio broadcasts the plaintive strains of an old Mandarin favourite from the 1930s. A woman's deep voice sings, "My love for you, unrequited / I'm chilled, like a winter's night without the moon / You won't turn your heart to me / Love's image hidden by the dark..."

I stop to listen to the music. Unrequited love. How it creates such a deep and penetrating chill. Unrequited love can destroy you if you let it. I recall Selim's text message. He loved someone who didn't love him back. Or so he said. Did that have to do with why he killed himself?

ONCE I'm back in my hotel room, I raid the mini fridge and climb onto the bed with a cold can of Tiger beer and Pringle's potato chips. Getting to be a habit, this Tiger beer thing. I channel surf but find it rather unsatisfying. TV off, I start to hum that old Mandarin song I heard in the *kopi tiam* on my walk back. I remember some of the lyrics from the days when it played often at the back of Cosmic Pulse. On slow afternoons when there were no customers to tend to, Hwi would switch on his little National transistor radio in the kitchen. He tuned in to the Hong Kong station, and we would be regaled with ballads and love songs, many of them originating from Shanghai in its heyday in the 1930s and '40s.

I sit cross-legged, back against the headboard. The bed is surprisingly firm, almost as hard as the futon I sleep on at home. I flip through *The Gay Science*. I randomly select one of the pages marked by a sticky note. My eyes are drawn to section 287, "Delight in Blindness":

> *My thoughts, said the wanderer to his shadow, should show me where I stand, but they should not betray to me where I am going. I love ignorance of the future and do not want to perish of impatience and premature tasting of things promised.*

I draw in a long, slow breath and release a hum of approval. I'm impressed by Nietzsche. The richness of experience is diminished when we try to anticipate or even control the unpredictable. It's that gravity-defying spirit all over again, that *Wissenschaft* Nietzsche was committed to. I'm jolted out of my reverie by the phone ringing on the side table.

"It's Adam."

"Oh, what's up?"

"I'm just outside the hotel, parking the car. Can I come up?"

"Why are you here?"

"I have something I must tell you."

A few moments later, his knock on the door sounds hesitant. I open the door to find a red-faced Adam with a pronounced smell of alcohol on his breath. The stink disgusts me. I back away as he sways unsteadily on his feet.

I let him enter but keep the door open, just in case. He stumbles to the armchair under the TV and sits down.

"Tell me what you have to say, and go. It's quite late."

"Doesn't being the husband of your first lover entitle me to special consideration?" He tries to hold my gaze with his, but I avoid his stare.

"I don't know what you mean."

He laughs. "I can see I'm unsettling you. Don't worry, I'm not going to hurt you." He raises his hands as if to reassure me, but his gesture doesn't give me any comfort. "I'm not a homo, okay? I just want you to know that. Just because both my wife and my son like people of the same sex...uh...you know what I mean?"

So Adam knew about his son. It takes him getting drunk to talk about this? I grit my teeth and say, "No, I don't. You're going to have to spell it out."

"I don't mind if you still want to sleep with my wife. I mean, help her get it out of her system. I don't care."

"What?"

"It's not the same with women."

"I'm having a hard time understanding what your point is."

"She's not happy. I don't know how to make her happy. And now Selim's dead..."

"I'm sorry, Adam."

"Of course women love each other. That's not rocket science. It's the attraction between men that's dangerous.

Whereas it's nice for men to know their wives are still attractive. I don't mind. You have my permission." Now his eyes seem to be looking past me, unfocused.

"You must leave now," I say, backing toward the door, wondering if I need to call the hotel staff for help.

Moving as if in slow motion, Adam drops his head into his hands. I hear his laboured breathing and wonder what he's going to do next. Then a strained sound emerges from his throat, as if he were an animal whining in pain. It seems a long time before he starts to cry.

"I don't want to hurt anyone . . . I just want . . ." But he doesn't say more. Can't, because he's gasping as he continues to weep.

"Adam, go home. You've been having a rough time of it."

"Why do I have to leave now?" He shakes his head, looking confused. "Oh, I don't know . . . you seem like a good person . . . loyal to Faridah, even though she left you."

I sigh loudly, not bothering to tone it down. I feel sorry for Adam, but at the same time, I wish he could just shut up and go home. This conversation is making me terribly irritated. I cross my arms over my chest.

"I need someone to confide in. There's something I feel terribly burdened by. People are so disappointed in me."

"Who?" I'm stunned by his sudden show of need.

"I get it all the time. They don't have to say. I can read their feelings. You're not the husband I wanted. Not the right kind of father. Why did God take our son away?"

"You're blaming God for taking Selim?"

"No. I mean the first one. The son that was stolen from us. Did I make a mistake, insisting that we give the next child the same name? Gabriel wasn't happy with me. Was that why he stopped using the Christian name I gave him? I tried to be a good father, but I had to discipline him. For his own sake."

I shudder at the phrase "For his own sake." Uttered with such confidence.

Adam looks pleadingly at me. "Believe me, I tried hard to show him I loved him, needed him."

I recoil, startled by the contrast in tone between his previous remark and this one, laden with vulnerability.

"Is that what made him want other men to hurt him? Is that it? You tell me!" He rises from his chair and grabs my left hand. I put my right hand lightly on his right arm and quickly palpate the skin near his elbow crease to locate *Qu Chi*, Pool at the Bend, on the large intestine meridian. I press down. Hard. Adam startles from the shock and releases his grasp. He reels, backing out into the hallway. He turns away and heads toward the elevator.

I LEAN hard against the closed door. Pause there for quite a while before I heave a sigh of relief and flop down on the chair.

While studying biology at U of T, I yearned to make sense of the world using logic and analysis. I had hoped I could tame mysteries that way. But even then, in my twenties, I already knew there were some experiences I couldn't explain or capture using that approach. Some part of me refused to compromise memories from my childhood by viewing the world so coldly. I couldn't abandon the memory of the strange vision I'd had, or what I had learned sitting with Mah-Mah as she consulted the Oracle.

Why do we humans insist on our habitual notions and behaviours, even when the evidence is right there in front of our eyes, suggesting that we view the world in a different way? Why do we resist evidence? Is it because of fear? Do we adore theories so much that we would willingly sacrifice experience for the sake of an elegant explanation?

Selim welcomed the unpredictable. He wanted to root himself in the present, not to compromise his joy of living in the moment. Experience over theory. But it seems that Adam is another kind of creature, one who prefers to cling to certain notions, even if those beliefs made his relationship with Selim fraught with difficulty and suffering. Some of his comments tonight were perplexing. He said he needed to discipline Selim for his own good, yet he admitted in the next breath that he needed his son. He uttered both statements with conviction. As if there were no other possible ways of viewing things.

Troubling. And what else was he implying? That his need for Selim made his son turn to other men to harm him? Or that Selim actually craved being disciplined by his father?

I try to put myself in Adam's place, try to imagine just what kind of crazy logic he might be operating under. He knew that Selim was gay. But he couldn't accept it. According to Faridah's account, he wouldn't talk about it. But now he has, when pissed drunk. He also said I could sleep with his wife. Help her "get it out of her system."

Fear makes people do and say crazy things.

I didn't know that their first son had been named Gabriel. Old Testament allusion. Gabriel, the messenger from God who prevented Abraham from slaying Isaac. The same angel who told Mary she would conceive Jesus.

I switch off the light on the side table and lie awake, trying to push aside the unpleasant thoughts. After what seems like too much time, I return in my mind to the ocean, and the lulling sound of waves against the sand.

twelve 脈

Finally, toward the end of Secondary One, in 1972, it was time for the annual school concert. On the stage at the morning assembly, we gathered in three groups: the Highs, the Lows and the Chorus. Stretched out in front of us was the whole school: girls sitting cross-legged on the parquet floor, a green sea of pinstriped blouses underneath pleated pinafores. The teachers sat in chairs lined up along the sides of the auditorium.

Faridah was standing to my left on stage. We were in the back row of the Low voices. She lightly touched my hand, then half-covered it with hers. I felt self-conscious, withdrew my hand and hid it in my pinafore pocket. I was nervous, never having been part of a public performance before. I thought of our kisses in my room and felt afraid that others would notice that we had something different happening between us. Just then, the girls in the Chorus began to sing out with great gusto.

> *You are a child of the universe*
> *no less than the trees and the stars;*
> *you have a right to be here*

Miss Rajah was smiling as she conducted us, mouthing the words while her eyes shone with fierce enthusiasm. As I recited my lines with the rest of the Lows, I felt a soft ache in my chest. The ache seemed to throb, extending to the corners of the auditorium.

I felt light, floating on the rhythm of the words. As if love could carry me anywhere I wanted, transport me beyond the mundane details, which were powerless to keep me chained.

WE WERE together for three years. I was counting on love. Counting on that energy to rescue me from Papa's abuse. Without knowing it, I had made Faridah the gatekeeper of my vitality.

The truth is, no one could have saved me then.

I think of trigraph 53, the one I never got. *Shen Zhu*, Assistance of the Spirits.

Mah-Mah assured me that such a time would come to pass. But when?

I gaze out at the ocean. At the ships in the far distance, further dwarfed by the brilliant sunlight. Those youthful voices that channelled "Desiderata" drift back to me, as if they're coming from a point beyond the visible horizon. Voices that were fervent with hope for the future. Now they're echoing within me, surrounded by the chatter of the people here for the memorial service.

Selim would have liked this, I think to myself. How thoughtful of Faridah to suggest holding the event here. He was fond of the ocean, often coming to Marine Parade to walk or swim.

We're a small group gathered under a gazebo, trying not to draw attention to ourselves. No one is sure if this is legal, this public meeting of eighteen people. Did Faridah and Adam have to apply for a permit to meet like this? The people here seem relaxed, mingling with one another before the actual proceedings start. It's a different gazebo than the one Faridah and Adam used for that Chinese New Year party in 2005, but it's much the same kind of structure, a rectangular pyramid sheltering four benches along the sides, with one in the middle, all of them poured concrete.

The strangest thing is to see Miss Rajah again after all these years. It was easy to recognize her, her former frame of five foot one now slightly diminished by age. But those eyes are unmistakable, possessing the same fiery gleam. She now sports a shorter haircut, the hair dyed a sleek jet black, the wrinkles radiating from her eyes the most pronounced clue to time's passing.

Adam plays music at a low volume from a ghetto blaster. A requiem called "Sanctus" by Maurice Duruflé. It was his choice. Violin strings precede the voices of boys and men, but the voices soon rise above the instrumental accompaniment, building toward a powerful *"hosanna in excelsis deo."*

I look around me as I listen to the music. I'm guessing that the middle-aged couple sitting next to Adam's mother are Adam's brother and sister-in-law. Adam bears a strong resemblance to his younger brother. I don't know many of the people here. Most are young, probably friends of Selim's. They're huddled together, sullen. A couple of them glance anxiously at Philip. Maybe looking for some reassurance.

Philip is dressed in a light blue long-sleeved shirt and black jeans, bare feet in sandals. Elbows on his legs, hunched forward. He keeps his head down, eyes concealed behind sunglasses.

Christina is quiet, staring at a framed photo of her brother, perched on the makeshift altar on the central concrete block. The photo is flanked by a vase of orchids and a small statue of Madonna with child. I catch her looking at her parents—one, then the other, back and forth. She looks anxious.

Adam tries to clear his throat, but his voice is hoarse and uncertain, in contrast to the confidence implied by his words. "All right, we should start."

We find places to sit on the four benches.

Adam continues, "We want to thank our family and friends and Gabriel's . . . Selim's . . . friends for being here. It's a simple event this afternoon. After all, we already had the formal service three weeks ago." He nods at Faridah and sits down.

I'm surprised at Adam's show of vulnerability, switching from the name he preferred to the one that was his son's choice. Here, in front of everyone. He didn't call his son by his Malay name last night in my hotel room. I wonder how he feels now about his behaviour. Wonder if he realizes how much he exposed of himself.

Still sitting, Faridah looks thoughtfully at the audience before she speaks. "Many of you know how much Selim disliked pretentious rituals. Isn't it ironic that it's only after he's gone that he gets to be honoured for his joyous and irreverent nature? I used to believe that parents needed to control their children. Too many times I panicked that I had a son whom I didn't understand, who was unruly and sometimes unpredictable. But now . . ." She pauses, looks down at her skirt and starts to pick at the frayed threads along the hem. She pulls hard, as if determined to remove the threads, but a couple end up lengthening instead. It's as if she's forgotten the rest of us, if only temporarily, urgently focused instead on completing this task. Finally, she looks up and resumes speaking, as if nothing had interrupted her line of thinking, ". . . I realize that Selim was the kind of person I never dared to be. Bravely unconventional. A spirit that couldn't be contained. Life seemed far too limiting for him."

Faridah stares at the pattern on her skirt. What does she see there? It's a batik pattern with purple and orange flowers set against a rose pink background. I wonder what she's thinking of when she describes her son as bravely unconventional. Is she thinking of his bondage practice?

A long silence follows Faridah's speech. I watch for signs of response from the others. Most eyes are downcast, with some awkward shifting of bodies, the crossing and uncrossing of legs. Adam's mother seems to shrink further into herself. Motionless, perhaps locked in shock.

After a long silence, a couple of Selim's male friends from university speak about their time together, somewhat bland accounts of eating junk food and staying up late cramming for exams or anguishing over favourite philosophers. Neither of them mentions Selim's fondness for Nietzsche.

Philip raises his hand to signal to Adam that he wants to speak. "I'm not one to make speeches. There's a lot I don't know how to express. I'm often worried I will say too much. Or something I will regret. All I can say is that I miss him terribly." He finishes abruptly, then stares at the ocean, looking lost.

Miss Rajah stands up, her posture showing confidence. "May I offer a few words? Of course there's reason for sadness. But this is also a chance to reflect on what persists despite the tragedy, to ask if there still remain reasons for gratitude. I hardly knew this young man. My association is more with his mother. I remember teaching Faridah at TKGS a long time ago. I'm touched by the way Faridah can celebrate her son's spirit. In fact, the way she just spoke reminds me of how she was as a lively and spirited teen. She should be proud she passed on some of that zest for living to Selim." She pauses and clears her throat. "I'd like to finish by quoting some lines from 'Desiderata': *Take kindly the counsel of the years, gracefully surrendering the things of youth. Nurture strength of spirit to shield you in sudden misfortune.*"

Waves of shock and recognition pass over Faridah's face. The words we uttered then reverberate now with the searing depth of her loss. That innocence—once so natural—has completely and irrevocably slipped away from us.

As soon as Miss Rajah sits down, Adam jumps up to announce that the service is over, and it's time for food and refreshments. I shift uneasily. Seems premature to end the service like this. It's as if Adam couldn't bear the intensity of Miss Rajah's words and had to escape the discomfort.

"Do you remember me?" Uncanny how shy I feel as I approach Miss Rajah.

"Why, of course, Natalie. The peculiar one. The last thing I heard was that you and your parents emigrated to Canada."

I'm pleased at the tone of genuine interest in her voice. "That's right."

She beams at me. "Are you happy?"

"Happier, yes."

"That's the most important thing, I believe. To be happy, no matter what." She meets my gaze uncompromisingly.

"There's a great line I heard somewhere, goes something like this: Would you rather be happy or would you rather be right?"

"You haven't changed much, Natalie." She smiles warmly.

Miss Rajah notices that Philip has come close, waiting to speak to me. She squeezes my hand gently, nods and then turns to talk to someone else.

Philip touches my elbow. "I know we haven't spoken, but I was wondering . . . do you have time to meet up tomorrow or the day after?"

I'm surprised, but I give him a quick nod. We arrange to meet in the Kampong Glam area the next day.

I walk down to the beach, thinking of the day Selim approached me about Cosmic Pulse as we looked out at the ocean. But it wasn't the same ocean, since water never stays static; everything has changed through the inevitable work of currents.

Hadn't I promised myself that I would never let anyone get too close? Then I fell for Faridah. To want love is to risk being hurt. To be flung about by the inexplicable needs of others. That's the kind of formula I lived by. I've shut myself up in a cave of numbness for such a long time.

I was wrong. I made a mistake. Now I'm coming to a different understanding.

I think of the way Adam was last night. Then there was that man in that Mandarin movie classic *Love Without End*.

To be closed is to be more vulnerable. I've been so fragile all these years. It takes strength to be open. Open so that I can experience the richness of life, and the truths that await my discovery. I want to be open, so that I no longer risk compromising the heart of my own needs.

I listened to the Dalai Lama on a telecast talk recently when he visited Toronto. He likened suffering to a vast ocean. The metaphor resonated with me. Suffering seems endless, stretching out in front of us into infinity. But there are ways—he said—to lessen that suffering. And those ways don't have to do with eliminating the turbulence of life, but involve riding the changing currents. Staying afloat.

I glance back at the others chatting under the gazebo. Under the brilliant early-afternoon sun, their shadows are pronounced, though stunted. I notice Miss Rajah saying goodbye to Faridah, clasping her hand in both of hers, then walking away.

There's no need for me to linger here. It would be especially awkward to interact with Adam and Faridah right now. I slip away without saying goodbye.

thirteen 脈

He wasn't supposed to be home so early. I heard his heavy footsteps. The main door into our living room clicked open then shut. His footsteps faded away and then came closer.

"You're shaking," Faridah whispered, looking at me with wide-eyed alarm.

"Quiet." I covered her mouth with my hand.

The door to my room rattled as Papa tried the knob.

"Open the door." His tone was plaintive, begging.

I raised my voice at him, "You can't come in!"

"Heng, why you home so early?"

Mum. Her voice drew near, sounding tense. His footsteps backed away from the door.

We stumbled out of bed, grabbed our clothes off the floor and hurriedly slipped back into our pinafores.

"What? Her friend in there too?" Papa's voice growled in response to Mum's comments. "Why she keep visiting our daughter? Secondary Four, and they still spend so much time together? Why they don't open door?"

"I got questions too. Why you coming home early more and more? I know you not happy at work. You fellows sit around here complaining. What else you not telling? Why you want to get into her room? Tell me!"

We rushed to the door to peek out between the cracks. Mum's profile was visible. The veins in her neck were showing, her muscles tense. Her eyes were widened in anger.

Papa's face was red and flushed. His eyes darted around our living room. I saw him fix his gaze on the steam iron cooling on the table. He walked toward it with a chilling deliberateness. What was he going to do? I panicked, unlatched the door and rushed out.

"Stop it!" I wedged my body between my parents just as he raised the iron above his head. I felt the dull heaviness descend on my shoulder. My legs buckled under me, and I fell to the floor.

The pain in my shoulder made it difficult to breathe. "No more," I gasped as I struggled up. I snatched the scissors from the far end of the table and staggered toward Papa. From behind me, I felt the firm hold of Mum's hands on my shoulders. But not firm enough to stop me.

I sunk the scissor blades into his right arm. The iron fell to the floor as Papa reeled back. I saw the gash on his arm and the slow appearance of blood. He stumbled, but managed to retrieve the iron. I blinked just as I felt a sharp blow against the side of my head. A chill came over me, and the room disappeared into a slate of whiteness.

When I came to, I couldn't move. I was on the floor, tied up. The ropes ate into my skin. I winced from the pain. My clothes were strewn all across the living room. I felt like crying, but all that came out of me were gasps, in rapid succession.

I heard my mother arguing with Papa downstairs in the courtyard. Their voices drifted up to me through the open windows. I felt utterly helpless. Ashamed and humiliated. Sweat poured out of me, trickling down from my forehead, stinging my eyes.

I was possessed by a fierce tremor. Couldn't stop. I felt as if I couldn't breathe. I recalled how Kong-Kong looked while having an asthmatic attack. What if my lungs failed me suddenly? Surely this was the way people felt just before taking their last breath. No one would hear me, be able to rescue me in time. The panic escalated.

"You stay out of this!" Papa's voice boomed.

I heard his footsteps on the stairs, approaching with a determined rhythm. I felt the strength of his rage as he dragged me to my feet, half-carrying, half-pushing me like a sack of potatoes down the stairs.

In the open courtyard, Mum and Faridah stood in the shade of the kitchen. Mum held tightly onto Faridah's arm.

"God saved your life in 1964, and what for? What kind of daughter? You are garbage!"

"Heng, please stop, I beg you!" Mum sobbed.

"Spare the rod and spoil the child. See what happens when you don't obey your father, huh?"

He pushed my bound body against the outer edge of the well. "You don't deserve to live! You…you…betrayed me." Tears streamed from his eyes as he stared at my body. Resting his gaze on my breasts and my sex, as if he were about to devour me.

I thought, *I don't want this*. My father's lust, his blind rage.

Faridah screamed and pleaded, "Stop, please!"

He looked back at her and shouted, "You! It's your fault. You corrupt my precious child. Mine…" He broke down and sobbed.

I couldn't speak. I wanted to say something, but no words came. He closed his fingers around my throat. I felt the air pushed out of me. My lungs hurt as my throat burned with the force of his grip. I started to gag.

Papa released his grip and pushed my head into the water. I felt the water rush into my mouth and sting my eyes. I disappeared into the pain. Lost all sense of my body. Then he lifted my head out of the water. I made sputtering noises, coughing violently. Felt on the brink of blacking out.

Once again he closed his hands around my throat,

poised to strangle me.

So this is it, I thought. *I'm going to die at my father's hands.*

But he came to an abrupt stop, hands still around my neck. I caught the look of fright in his eyes. What had happened? He seemed to have seen something that alarmed him. He was staring into the water past my head. Something in the well? Or overhead, reflected in the water below? He released his hold on me and backed away.

The silence was stifling. It offered no peace, no "Desiderata." The Natalie I was before that moment disappeared. I felt a collapse inside as she abandoned me.

It seemed an eternity as I endured Papa's laboured breaths, Mum's chilling silence and Faridah's sobs. I made a vow to myself, as I hunched over the edge of the well, the ropes burning their rough presence into my skin, that one day I would make Papa pay for everything he had done to me. I would dedicate the rest of my life to hating him. This was the last time he could possess me. I would make sure of that.

AH SEE and Hwi untied me, their hands strong and reassuring. I felt numb, unable to speak or even cry. I felt the soft presence of a flannel sheet being wrapped around me from behind.

"What are you doing, Ah Mak?" Mum asked hoarsely as my grandmother ordered the two servants to help me to the back room.

I was still trembling and felt faint, so I rested my forehead on the table. I felt someone gently touch my hands and turn them over so my palms were facing up. The wooden disks dropped into my hands.

"Shake them," Mah-Mah said, with a tone that was urgent yet resolute.

My hands wouldn't stop trembling. I lifted my gaze to meet my grandmother's eyes. They were fired with an intensity that compelled me to obey. Without resistance, I shook the wooden chips in my cupped hands briefly before dropping them onto the table.

"Number 52, *Chien Chang*, Wickedness Excelling," announced Mah-Mah.

She opened up the booklet and read it aloud in Mandarin. "Cut off, separated. Many obstacles. Whatever is done cannot succeed." She shut the book before continuing, "But there will come a time when this can be changed. That is Tao."

Faridah was hiding in the corner of Mah-Mah's room, shaking and crying. That was the last sound I heard before I passed out again.

fourteen 脈

Number 197 is a double-decker bus that cruises down Marine Parade Road then meanders through the Kallang area. Soon the bus is whizzing along Nicholl Highway, the air conditioning on full blast, in contrast to the muggy atmosphere outside. I peer out at the view, the ocean on the left, towers and skyscrapers on the right. The merlion sculpture on Marina Bay comes into view, endlessly spewing water out of its mouth back into the ocean. Whoever thought up this hybrid symbol—combining the story of Sang Nila Utama spotting lions on the island in the eleventh century with the Western myth of the mermaid—was a marketing genius.

In contrast, past the end of the new highway stand the remnants of Clifford Pier: all boarded up and no longer the busy international passenger terminal it used to be. Degeneration *is* the way of the Tao. I get off at the next stop, on Shenton Way just across from Lau Pa Sat, Telok Ayer Market.

I wind my way through the smaller streets behind the market. Next to the Thian Hock Keng temple, there's a plaque describing the history of the area. The tone is matter-of-fact in declaring that the area had been a Malay settlement, but when the British arrived in 1819, it was given over to the Chinese.

I'm sure Selim's forefather Munshi Abdullah must have been appalled at that decision, likely initiated or approved by Raffles. How glib historical plaques can be, glossing over so much, all in the service of presenting "facts" in as neutral a tone as possible.

At the temple gates, I look through the open doors. In the courtyard stands a large incense urn bearing the carvings of elephant bodies along its base. The smoke rises up and permeates the air. Staring past the smoke into the dark interior, populated with altars and worshippers, I start to feel drowsy. Despite this, I walk in, slowly approaching the inside of the temple.

A strange vision starts to form above the main altar. A body hangs from the ceiling, but the face is not Selim's. It's mine. I gasp, staggering back.

"Mind where you going, huh?"

I feel a pair of hands push against my back, preventing me from falling. I turn around to see the consternation on the young woman's face. Apologizing quickly, I exit the temple.

I walk briskly away, toward Chinatown. Take deep breaths as I try to reassure myself. It's gone, that awful hallucination. Whatever it was. Just a product of my own imagination. My fear. I head along Clarke Quay.

My heart continues to beat fast. Why? Where is the danger?

I look across the river at the looming presence of the OUB towers. Twin towers that remain standing. In front of them is the Botero sculpture, near where I met Selim that day in 2005. I stare at its form, dwarfed by distance.

I'm remembering too much, the memories flooding back all at once. I can feel the emotion rising in my throat, clogging it like debris. Feeling choked. Can't hold it in any longer. I lean over the railing, my tears falling into the dirty, polluted river. I feel like throwing up. I'm no longer the same person who met Selim that day on the other side of the river.

When I've calmed down a bit, I read the plaque next to me, describing Raffles' landing. History. Cold lines etched permanently in stone. They can never replace the pulse and spirit of experience, nor the pulse and spirit of those who have left. I sigh at the sound of another *tongkang* passing by on the water.

Wake up.

I turn around, shuddering. A chill passes through me. I'm sure I didn't imagine the words. But all I see are the indifferent looks of strangers passing me by. No one except me knows that I've seen a ghost. The ghost that was once me.

I DECIDE to browse in the shops at People's Park Complex. There are numerous shops selling DVDs. It isn't difficult to find a copy of the original *Godzilla* movie, called *Gojira* in Japanese. Selling for only eight Singapore dollars. I walk along South Bridge Road until I locate an Internet café. I put on headphones and, with a single click, enter the world of a twentieth-century mythical monster.

Godzilla, proclaims Professor Yamane, the paleontologist in charge of the investigation, is a cross between a marine animal and a terrestrial one. Hence capable of existing in both domains. Yamane says Godzilla has surfaced because he was exposed to massive amounts of radiation, and the exposure displaced him from his natural habitat in the depths of the ocean. At one point, a journalist asks the professor how he knows Godzilla's sudden appearance has to do with the atomic bomb, and Yamane answers that traces of strontium-90 were found in the sand where Godzilla had been, strontium-90 being a radioactive material generated from an atomic bomb.

I'm noticing aspects of the movie I don't remember from the first time I watched it. I don't think the American version went into such detail about the presence of strontium-90. It is so much clearer in the original film, the link between the destructiveness of the monster and the atomic bomb, a creation of humanity.

I'm struck by the character Dr. Serizawa. Tall and handsome, he's marked by a black patch over his right eye. He has a dark secret he shares with Emiko, his fiancée. He demonstrates the power of the Oxygen Destroyer, a machine he has created that would destroy all the oxygen in the cells of living organisms, thus disintegrating them. He demonstrates the action of the Oxygen Destroyer in a fish tank. All of the fish are annihilated. Only their skeletal forms remain. The shadowy, tortured profile of Serizawa is a contrast to Emiko's pale, terrified face.

Lieutenant Ogata wishes to convince Serizawa to use the Oxygen Destroyer against Godzilla. A debate ensues between the two men. Serizawa is afraid that if the Oxygen Destroyer were to be used even once, politicians would want to use it again. It is Ogata who insists that there is a difference between Serizawa's fears and the very real threat of Godzilla, which *is* reality.

Ogata is very much the kind of hero that popular culture worships: decisive and confident. When he asks what they are to do with the horror they are faced with, there isn't a trace of doubt in his demeanour. He doesn't falter in his conviction that Godzilla must be destroyed.

Serizawa, on the other hand, is a completely different kind of man. He's plagued by doubt. He worries about the implications of his actions. And he is certainly not as pretty as Ogata, being marked by a patch over one eye. When Serizawa is confronted by the tremendous devastation wrought by Godzilla, he relents and ultimately decides to use his weapon, but only once.

Possessed by his love for humanity, Serizawa eliminates everything that would enable someone else to make another Oxygen Destroyer—including himself. He cuts the hose to his air supply at the bottom of the ocean floor so that he is annihilated along with the monster when he activates his Oxygen Destroyer.

After the movie has ended, I look around at my companions in the Internet café. What a common scene in the twenty-first century. A group of strangers gathered together in a public space to stare at computer screens and engage with virtual reality. Peace, affluence, health—how easy it is to take these for granted. So many of us in North America are comfortably distanced from the horrific suffering of others.

I take a few deep breaths. Emiko had fallen in love with Ogata. Not only did she leave Serizawa, she also betrayed her promise to him to keep the existence of the Oxygen Destroyer a secret. Did the power of betrayal and unrequited love spur him on to sacrifice himself?

No, that doesn't fit with what I just saw. It had nothing to do with sentimental romance. Serizawa was motivated by his moral conscience. He felt strongly that his life— and the loss of it—had to mean something for the sake of humanity. What a selfless motivation.

I whisper under my breath, "Wow, this hadn't occurred to me until now."

Serizawa. Selim. Did Faridah's son sacrifice his life for some cause he deemed worthy? Until this moment, I had assumed it was despair that led Selim to kill himself.

I rest my elbows on the computer table and cup my face in my hands. I feel a dull, throbbing pain overtake my forehead. My hands are chilled, a contrast to the heat emanating from my head.

LOST in the thick of the crowd, I find myself jostling with shoppers to look at the myriad temptations around us, the flash of sensory pleasures infinitely alluring in a superficial way. But deeper and more insistently embedded in my consciousness are scenes and words from the movie.

After a late lunch of wonton *mee*, I walk along New Bridge Road, heading north, past shopping complexes interspersed with office buildings. Turning right at Upper Hokkien Street, I spy a few older HDB government flats in an area where, one hundred years ago, brothels would have lined the side streets. Instead of its former seediness, the street has been tidied up, with the old façades carefully restored to attract tourists.

I continue on South Bridge Road, the wide road zooming with multi-lane traffic, flanked on either side by more malls and hotels, including the Adelphi, where my parents held their wedding reception almost fifty years ago.

Farther ahead, I pass by St. Andrew's Cathedral and run into the after-work rush of commuters in front of the City Hall MRT station.

Ten minutes later, I reach the lush yet controlled beauty of the courtyard garden in the heart of Raffles Hotel. I pause on a wrought-iron bench and look up to the rooms on the second storey. Rooms once occupied by Joseph Conrad, Somerset Maugham, Ava Gardner and Charlie Chaplin.

It's restful sitting here, despite my longstanding refusal to romanticize. History has been sanitized—suffering and carnage concealed under the mantle of creeping ivy. It's not common knowledge that no Asians were allowed on these grounds until 1930, nearly fifty years after the hotel opened. How many people of this current generation of youths know that when the Japanese occupied Singapore from 1942 to 1945, they named Raffles Hotel *Syonan Ryokan*? *Syonan* meaning "Light of the South," their name for Singapore, and *Ryokan* meaning a Japanese inn. Such euphemistic denial that the hotel had served as a transit camp for British prisoners of war.

When Lord Mountbatten and his naval fleet entered Singapore on September 4, 1945, and demanded surrender from the Japanese troops on the island, three hundred Japanese soldiers refused to surrender and killed themselves with grenades at *Syonan Ryokan*. Perhaps even on this very spot where I am now resting. How things have changed: many of the guests at Raffles these days are tourists from Japan.

The atmosphere, the connection to other meanings, lead me to softly recite Conrad out loud, as if Kong-Kong were speaking through me:

Life knows us not and we do not know life. We don't know even our own thoughts ... Faith is a myth and beliefs shift like mists on the shore; thoughts vanish; words, once pronounced, die; and the memory of yesterday is as shadowy as the hope of to-morrow ...

I imagine Conrad must have been lonely. Only someone who has travelled widely and fearlessly in his imagination, and has witnessed human cruelty, could write such words.

fifteen 脈

The Bugis MRT station is the closest one to Kampong Glam. The station is packed with people. As I exit, I spot some schoolchildren holding small flags, and others dressed up quite colourfully. I had forgotten. It's National Day.

I recognize Philip, leaning against a wall, reading *The Straits Times*.

"Philip," I offer my hand.

"Aunty, glad you agreed to come." He folds up the paper and shakes my hand with a firm and warm grasp.

I smile wistfully at being called Aunty yet again. One generation apart: is that all it takes to earn respect?

We walk past the Golden Landmark Hotel and take a right on Arab Street. We're soon at the traffic lights, the gold domes of the Sultan Mosque diagonally across from us.

"I don't remember any of this," I remark, scanning the rows of shops as we stroll along Muscat Street.

"This area has been recently revitalized."

The cobblestoned pedestrian street is predominantly flanked by clothing shops. I notice a bookstore next to a backpackers' hostel and gesture to Philip that I would like to go in to have a look. Philip shrugs nonchalantly and remains out on the street to have a smoke.

It's almost 5:00 p.m., and one of the wooden doors has already been inserted into its groove, signalling that they're about to close.

A haunting sound greets me as I enter the small store. Male voices, energetic and impassioned, chant with an urgent pulse that's electrifying. The CD cover is displayed on the counter, along with a translation of the composer's inspiration: "I was suddenly paralyzed down one side of my body by a stroke. I decided to compose this ode, the Burdah . . . I fell asleep, and in a dream, I saw the Blessed Prophet. He moved his noble hand across my face, and placed his cloak upon me. When I awoke, I found that I had recovered my health."

The sound of unified voices stretches itself above me, a vast and pervasive presence. Very intense, a fervent paean that celebrates being healed.

"Let's go eat." I wave my hand at Philip as I return to the pavement outside.

He takes me down Kandahar Street to Sabar Menanti, which is bustling with customers who compete to order food from the display of *nasi padang* choices behind the glass. I point at fish and okra in curry, sambal long beans and finally, *achar* pickles. Philip chooses beef *rendang* and *sayur lodeh*. We both also order glasses of *teh tarik*.

We choose a table away from others, out of earshot. But we hardly speak as we eat our food. It's only when we are left with our glasses of sweet, milky tea that Philip begins.

"I asked to meet with you because I can't stand it anymore." Philip's voice is shaky. "I know that you and Selim had an important connection . . . I guess it's okay . . ."

"You can talk to me, Philip," I try to reassure him.

His face betrays a great deal of emotion. Waves of feeling that are inexpressible through words. He sips his tea, visibly shaken. "Aunty, it's too painful to bear this alone. I think I can trust you. You and Selim's mother were very close once. Selim told me." He nods awkwardly at me, then adds, "Yes, okay, here goes."

I nod in response, sensing I need to be patient with Philip.

We listen to the imam call out the evening prayers. The solitary voice sounds reassuring. It's a voice that reveals a certain kind of strength. I may not understand what he's saying, but I can easily feel the power of his commitment.

"Selim trusted you, so I'm going to take a big risk and tell you something very important. Just because I think he would want you to know."

I put down my hot glass, and stare at him, waiting.

"I know everything," he whispers.

"Yeah?"

"Everything. Including why Selim killed himself."

"But you haven't shared it with anyone else?"

"You'll understand once you see this." He pulls out a tattered envelope with a couple of sheets of paper folded inside.

"This is a note he slipped under my pillow. The night we . . . we last had sex. Before he went home. He must have written that note at an earlier time. Goes to show how prepared he was, waiting for the right opportunity."

I swallow hard. I had suspected they were lovers, but now I know for sure.

Philip gestures to me to sit next to him, as if he wants to guard me, or perhaps shield the contents of the letter from other eyes. My hands tremble slightly as I start to read silently.

Dear friend,

I know you'll be angry with me. It was either I do it here or at home. It's stupid to risk your reputation by dying here with you. Don't remain angry. I hope you'll be able to forgive me not too long from now. Don't hold bitterness in your heart. Remember, I'm just another flawed human being. So everyone praises me for being so smart. Since when is a smart person not allowed his vulnerability? Intelligence doesn't go far enough to diminish the impact of a wound. I sure found that out. I don't know what can.

We've had our moments of great happiness. Good enough, yeah? But life is not proving purposeful enough. I feel lost. Why am I doing what I'm doing? I'm not sure anymore.

You of all people know my deepest secrets. You know what drives me to risk myself. Every time I managed to escape, to survive, I felt a growing restlessness after the initial high. You know I'm one to be insatiably curious. You've never begrudged me my other lovers and my need for adventure. My feelings fascinate me. Why are human beings never satiated? I do get morose when I think too much! I keep reaching the same dead-end place, pardon the perverse pun.

I thought my father would have realized how much I love him despite all the wrong-headed things he's done in the name of good parenting. My fantasy proceeds in this way: he would suddenly come to his senses and accept me in his deepest soul. Then he would stop all these ridiculous angry tirades against me. You know how he's treated me. Didn't anyone ever tell parents they're responsible for their children, not the other way around?

It is undeniable that I've enjoyed much pleasure in Kinbaku. Yet those pleasures only leave me craving more. What's the point of a temporary escape?

No matter where I turn, I can't escape him. Not literally, of course. You know he stopped bothering me a decade ago. Ever since I turned sixteen. So, from age nine to sixteen. A hell of a long time. Yeah, it sure helped that I got a whole lot stronger than him. He became afraid I would harm him. So what? The shadow of his crime darkens our household. His violence, the perverted desire that he won't name. A shadow my mother has not dared to name. She would rather think that her husband simply needed to be close to the son who survived. I know she's quite terrified of the truth. But I don't blame her. It's just too awful for a mother to contemplate. She's been so bloody miserable.

Even with all the ugliness, you know that I can see how tortured he's been. I see the beauty in him, the one who longs to be loved. Who never recovered from losing his first Gabriel. I mean, apart from the sex, it was because he let me witness his grief that I became so powerfully connected to him.

But what's the meaning of that connection? When it's based on an absence? What a paradox. I could never make it up to him, could never assuage his grief. There's no reason I should continue anymore, a stupid stand-in for my dead brother. My life mocks me. Every minute I live, I collude in a lie. My father never forgave me for being the son who survived. How twisted human logic can be, that I would have to bear that burden.

You make sure you share this with my mom's friend, Natalie. I want her to know. I'm relying on you to tell her, since I won't be able to. She knows what it's like, to love someone who won't—can't—love you back. That father

from whom we can never receive unconditional love. Im-
possible to ask for something that won't be given freely. So
there you have it. I've had enough.

At the very bottom of the page, Selim had signed it Benkulen Bound.

I raise my head from reading and look at Philip. I had feared this, had not dared to fully admit to myself what I suspected.

Philip avoids my gaze, choosing to look into the distance for quite a while. He puts his sunglasses back on.

I follow his gaze, toward the park across from us. Three pigeons are basking in the sun. I take a deep breath. There is no symbolic act that would make enough of a difference right now. Nothing can be done to bring Selim back.

I feel a tight weariness around my eyes as I continue to watch the pigeons. Unbearably beautiful sunlight, casting shadows against the soft grey of the pigeons' bodies, the rings of iridescence around their tender necks gleaming green and purple in the light, the two bars on each wing the marker of this common variety, *Columba livia*, rock pigeon.

"Did Adam ever know Selim was with you?"

"Yeah, he found out. There was a big scene between them."

"How did he find out?"

"He walked in on Selim and me making out in Selim's room. That was in early July. Mr. Khoo broke down and cried, saying he was heartbroken that his son would not want to marry and have children. He slapped Selim's face, and I jumped up to punch Uncle, but Selim prevented me."

I can't conceal the feelings of shock and anger. And how powerful a statement it is that a strong young man like Selim refused to retaliate.

I reach out to touch the back of Philip's hand. My skin so pale in contrast to his. He doesn't pull his hand away but lets me cover it with mine, as I struggle to find the words. What is it I really want to say? That he needs to forgive Adam? How could I possibly say that to him right now? It would sound far too trite and heartless.

"You need . . . some kind of release . . . to free yourself. It will be difficult. It will take a long time."

He clears his throat, coughing slightly. Tears run down his face, his eyes hidden behind the dark shades.

"Why have the police been so casual about the investigation?"

"It was a known fact . . . among some . . . about Selim's practices. They looked the other way because they had such fondness and respect for him."

"What about his cellphone? I assumed the police would have contacted me if they'd found it?"

Philip removes his sunglasses, eyes red from crying, and manages a smile. "Selim thought of that. He left it with me, next to the note. Must be his cellphone got lost, right? Disappeared into the Singapore River?"

"Another of the river's secrets."

THE lantern lights in front of the restaurants form a jagged, shifting line as the breeze moves through Boat Quay. Nonchalant strollers and manic seekers swarm through the sweltering humid night, buzzing with the throb of disco music.

I've found my way to the Asian Civilizations Museum. Looking up, it's hard to see much of the starry night. They're there, nonetheless, barely visible. Hidden by an opaque mist. I walk away from the street lamps. Behind the museum, at a darker, unlit corner, I catch a glimpse of Orion's Belt, the three stars I learned to identify as a child.

I try to imagine Kong-Kong as a young man, set off on a ship from Shanghai, on the outside deck one evening, looking up at the night sky. Did he notice Orion, the hunter in the sky? My grandfather the dreamer, who, recalling that feeling of mystery, later invented an intriguing name for his herbal shop.

Cosmic Pulse. The pulse of the universe. The pulse of the vast world of stars embodied in the microcosmos of the body.

I return to the edge of the river and look across at the Botero sculpture, details of its surface and form lost in the night.

I take my pulses on both wrists while, behind me, a group of young men and women, in their Junior College uniforms, emerge from the Arts Building, perhaps having just attended an event there.

I turn my attention back to those stars above, recalling some of the myths I read about in my acupuncture courses.

The *shen* spirits, who come to human beings from the stars, are believed to be the most refined, exquisite form of yang energy, the active and initiatory aspect of *qi* in the universe. *Shen* are likened to birds that fly upwards or flee the human body if the yin energies fail to entice them to reside in the hollow of the heart space. If these precious wild birds flee the heart, the light of the *shen* will no longer be there to guide and inform the movements of *qi*, the life force, in the person. Such a person shows the signs of feeling lost, lacking purpose in life.

The *zhi* spirits constitute the water element in the lower body. They are the ones who must entice the *shen* to remain in the body. It is yin energy in the body that must compel yang energy to return.

Someone with my training could describe Selim's loss of purpose as a loss of yin energies. A lack of nourishment from the activities of his life. He felt empty because the precious wild birds of his spirit had no home in the heart space of his body.

I walk back to the water's edge and stare at the shifting darkness below. Water, the shape shifter. The transformational element whose depths nurture all manner of creatures.

In the twenty-first century, instead of a singular, easily identifiable monster rising from the depths to threaten our world, there are instead the churnings of a troubled earth and ocean, the consequence of human interference. If the pull of the ocean is disturbed, what will become of us, those who rely on it?

I SIT in the dark of my hotel room, letting the feelings of sadness, then horror, pass through me. Spend a few minutes doing some acupressure on myself. Desperately in need of some distraction, I switch on the TV. Just in time to catch a rebroadcast of the prime minister's National Day message from the night before, delivered from the top floor of the National Library. First time this has happened, the PM delivering his message from the library.

The top floor, the pinnacle. How Confucian. I think of the ancient Chinese traditions in which emperors ascended sacred mountains to conduct rituals, proving to others their rightful place in the cosmos, proving they were chosen by Heaven.

The prime minister's speech starts out with a list of all the excellent achievements Singapore and its citizens have accomplished. He reports on the economic growth and productivity of the country. How different his style is from his father's. In the early days, our first prime minister emphasized Singapore's vulnerability at the hands of Communists. How brilliant Lee Kuan Yew was, to portray

Communist presence as compromising the economic welfare of the citizenry. He made the Communist threat sound ominous enough that people willingly trusted his charismatic leadership to save them.

After the PM's speech, highlights are shown from today's National Day Parade, held at Marina Bay. I love the burst of red as thousands of spectators unfurl fabric at the same time. Wow, talk about patriotism. Then the sky is streaked by the quick flight of F-16 fighter jets, the flare of their jets like tails dragged across the darkening sky. Makes me think of the mythological dragons in Chinese folklore, powerful creatures that ruled the skies and seas.

Next up, the song and dance performances. The commentator describes them as depicting the five elements: earth, fire, sea, sky and people. Very different from the five elements I know from Traditional Chinese Medicine. *What happened to wood, metal and water?* I wonder.

Following this is a flamboyant display of a giant water screen, onto which images of flickering flames and streams of bubbles are projected, a visual illusion acting as a backdrop for dances on the steel platform-stage. Very grandiose. Reminds me of those flashy Broadway musicals of the '50s.

The loud double ring of the telephone startles me. I look around the room, the spell now broken. I switch off the TV and pick up the phone.

"Long distance," the man at the reception desk chimes cheerily.

A click and then Michelle's voice comes over the

phone, a barely controlled quiver. "Natalie, it's Michelle."

"Hey, how are you?"

"Couldn't sleep. I have some bad news. My dad suffered a mild heart attack yesterday."

"Is he . . ."

"He's in stable condition now, thank goodness."

"What about you?"

"I'm upset but okay. I took yesterday and today off. I'll have to wait and see what the doctors say later today."

"I wish I were there," I whisper, as a memory of Mr. Woo lying face up on my acupuncture table flashes through my mind.

"Only three more days, my love, before you get back—I've missed you terribly. How are you?"

"A bit dazed, actually."

"Why? Tell me what's been happening over there."

"I just learned something troubling from Philip, Selim's best friend. Lover, actually."

"Oh?"

"Selim left him a long suicide note. Which explains a lot."

"What did it say?"

"I'll tell you when I see you."

"No, tell me now."

"In brief? Selim's father sexually abused Selim as a child, until he was sixteen."

I hear the sound of Michelle's breathing in the silence that ensues. Her breaths grow longer and louder until she blurts out, "Fuck."

"I know. It was awful to learn about it. Lots of things are starting to make sense to me." I need more time to sit with these revelations. Then maybe, much later on, I might be ready to tell Michelle about the connections between my past and Selim's.

"Does Faridah know?"

"Don't think so."

"Are you ... are you ... going to talk to her about it?"

"I don't know," I reply, sighing loudly.

We talk some more about her father, then say goodbye. I put on my headphones and listen to music on my iPod. There's a song I have in mind, "Wang Bu Liao" from the movie *Bu Liao Qing, Love Without End*.

Wang bu liao, wang bu liao ni de ai
Wang bu liao ni de cuo

"I can't forget, can't forget your love, I can't forget your wrongs." Intense and dramatic. Infused with melancholy and longing.

I know the song has come to mind because of what's going on. A song can say so much, touch the deepest truths. I listen to the song countless times. It's as if the repetition is helping me to trace what has disappeared, what is constantly in the act of disappearing.

Selim's note is a trace, a peculiar ghostly return. I now know what he wanted me to know.

I see why Selim was drawn to the story of my life. He was such a good listener. Quite exceptional, because he must have heard not only what his mother was telling him, but also the implications between the lines. He heard what she could not. I never told her about being sexually abused by my father. But her son heard it, because of his own experiences. His psyche resonated with the implication of my father's rage at discovering that Faridah and I were lovers. No wonder he wanted Philip to share the note with me.

He must have forgiven his father. I could hear it in his note. He refused to demonize Adam, for he longed to be loved by him. Longed to be touched. Truly and deeply, without taint.

It's time to turn to the Oracle. I place the book on the bed, facing north, then cup all twelve wooden chips in my hands. I can feel Mah-Mah's presence in the texture of these chips, the energy of her hands now residing in my palms. I rattle the chips for about a minute as I think of the question I wish to put to the Oracle. Something about meeting up with Faridah tomorrow. I know: I will ask if it will be useful to share some of what I learned from Philip or whether I should refrain.

I finally release the chips, letting them fall between me and the Oracle. I arrange the rows according to the chips that display symbols facing up. Four in the top row, for Heaven; one in the middle, for Humanity; and three for Earth, in the bottom row.

I consult the table at the back of the book. Number 51: Beneficial Friends. How odd, to obtain the trigraph that precedes Wickedness Excelling. The name of this trigraph is striking. Friends who would be beneficial to each other must surely be guided by sincerity. In reading the commentary, I realize that the Oracle is indicating that the action to be taken must be guided by one's heart. What is my heart's intention, then? I will wait to see what happens tomorrow.

sixteen 脈

"I'd like you to take this with you," says Faridah, passing *The Gay Science* back to me.

The canary is silent. It's mid-afternoon. Not as humid today. Noises from the street filter in: beeping sounds of a car compete with the syncopated beat of a Cantonese song. Faye Wong's quirky singing voice, backed by the dreamy sounds of a synthesizer keyboard. It's music that encases one in a bubble of ethereal presence. But what happens when the bubble bursts?

I accept the book from Faridah, and consider how to pose the first question. "I've been wondering how much you knew about Selim's life outside the family."

"If you mean, did I know he and Philip were lovers, the

answer is yes," she answers resolutely, but her eyes are downcast, as if ashamed.

"Why didn't you mention . . ." Then I realize how presumptuous I am. After all, we haven't been close in ages.

"There's no point talking about it, is there? Adam blames me."

"For what?"

"For Selim's so-called degenerate ways."

"I'm disgusted at Adam's—" I feel the heat flush my face. I want to tell her everything, to fling it all out into the open.

"Do you think it's been easy all these years? If you only knew half of what's been going on . . ."

She gets up from the sofa and walks out to the balcony. Faye Wong is still singing, asking why her man loves another. Faridah folds her arms across her chest and looks out. It seems a long time before she turns around to talk to me.

"I know this doesn't make sense, but I do blame myself for Selim's death. If I hadn't been . . . if I didn't have those feelings for you . . . life would have been very different. I wouldn't have told Selim those stories about you . . ."

". . . and he wouldn't have become gay? Is that what you're implying?"

"I don't know. I'm all muddled up."

The canary begins to sing. The hot breeze lifts the curtains, an uneasy flow of air that provides little relief.

She adds, "I'm worried about Adam. I think he's seriously unravelling."

"Yeah, well . . ." So tempting, but I must refrain.

"He's never gotten over the loss of our first child. There were so many nights he would go to Selim's room and cry there, lying next to his son."

"You saw that?"

"Yes, I did."

"What did you think of it?"

"I could see . . . well, that the loss changed him. I understood that. After all, it was devastating for me too. But Adam has never been the same since then. He . . . he . . . sort of shut down emotionally. Just couldn't be close to me."

"You've been living with this kind of loneliness for your entire marriage?" I shake my head in disbelief. Tragic. It's not the first time I've heard of this happening, people remaining in loveless relationships. But Faridah? Why?

"This is going to sound weird, but . . ."

I look at her quizzically, wondering what she will say next.

". . . I felt jealous. You must think this horrible, but I was upset at how much he relied on Selim for emotional support when he should have . . ."

". . . turned to you instead."

Faridah's face collapses into a vulnerable expression, exposed and raw for the depth of her sadness and loss. The afternoon sun slants in, casts shadows of the birdcage onto her body. She blinks at the light hitting her face.

She could see Adam's grief. Saw too that he went to Selim for companionship. Felt the loss of his love, but somehow it must have been too much to see what else was happening. She could have read her own jealousy in a different way, realized what her intuition was telling her. But she didn't do that. Stopped short of discovering the dark secret. Selim was right. She couldn't bear to face the truth.

She unfolds her arms and returns to the living room. Sits down next to me and speaks again, looking me straight in the eye, "That's right. Adam and I haven't been happy together. I thought, I thought . . . you know, you're supposed to stay with the one you married. I know that's old-fashioned, a rather horrible cliché, but there were the kids to think of . . ."

"And now?" I tilt my head, listening to the song of the canary. It has resumed singing.

"I'm leaving Adam," she proclaims, with a heavy sadness. Still looking directly into my eyes.

"God, that's a huge step. Takes a lot of courage."

"With Selim's death . . . I think that has led me to see what I need to do for myself. That speech I made at the memorial service? Well, I heard what I was saying to myself. I need to live more courageously. I let my parents' needs dictate my life. Or rather, my ideas of what I should do. Be respectable, get married. Don't let the miscarriage stop me. Have more children. Misguided, maybe. But that was how I was then. How naive of me."

"Yeah, I remember how adamant you were about making your parents happy."

"I risked my own happiness without realizing it. At the beginning and now. To miscarry was very hard, but to lose a son who grew up to become a wonderful young man…" She places her hand on her chest and shakes her head as tears well up. "I have a sweet daughter who's very messed up and unable yet to figure it out. And I've allowed Adam's unhappiness to get in the way of my personal fulfillment. Ironically, it's my brave, wild Selim who has inspired me. His need to take such a drastic step…whatever it was that motivated him, I'll always be angry that he took himself away from us like that. Without any thought for how we would all be affected. But then…but then…"

"…his action led to you finally making this choice."

"Yeah. Mysterious and upsetting at the same time."

I breathe out a large sigh, absorbing the enormity of what Faridah has shared. Selim would be happy, I think, to know this. That his mother is about to take this step to extricate herself from an unhappy marriage. He would be also gratified to know that he played a role in releasing her.

I place my hand over hers, resting on the sofa between us. Adjusting my breathing to be in sync with hers. My brave friend. She is finally returning to herself. I am moved by witnessing this transformation in her.

What would be the point in telling her about Selim's note to Philip? In disclosing the horrible details of Adam's abuse? If she couldn't handle seeing the truth, and Selim never wanted to tell her, then so be it.

I look into her eyes. I see an image of myself reflected in them. We were never really separated. We are deeply embedded in each other's memory. We were merely lost for a while. It's been hellish for her to lose Selim, but to discover why he chose to kill himself? That would be utterly devastating. She may not know all the facts, but at least she has named the truths. The truth of Adam's unhappiness and his distance from her. The way he turned to Selim for solace. Last and most important, the pressing truth she can't afford to ignore: the need to extricate herself from the lie she has been living.

What does my heart desire? Simply this: to see Faridah finally doing what she wants, to see her happy.

"I want to thank you for coming here."

"I'm glad I came."

"Selim was right. Reconnecting with you has brought some . . . what is the word?"

"Healing? Too cliché?"

She laughs quietly. "Yes. But clichés are sometimes true."

"In this case, it could well be the right word." I smile at her, grateful for the lightness that's still possible after all that has happened.

"When is your flight tomorrow?"

"1:30."

"I'll drive you to the airport."

"No, it's okay. I'll take a cab." I hate airport farewells, would not want to say goodbye to her there.

Faridah shrugs, looks away from me, so I can only see her profile. Is she listening to the sounds of romantic longing rise up from the blaring stereo outside? Faye Wong being replayed in an endless loop by an obvious fan. Does she understand the Cantonese lyrics? Maybe she doesn't need to understand the words to feel the emotional undertones of the song.

"You haven't told me much about your life in Toronto. I'm sorry, I haven't been in the right state of mind to ask... to listen..."

"It's okay. We can talk about my life some other time."

"Promise?" She smiles tenderly at me, a gleam in her eyes.

That gleam. I remember it so well. Why is it that I haven't been able to forget? How is it that love can be activated just like that? That pulse of electrical stimulation to the brain, but how mysterious its origins. I feel a surge of emotion rise to my throat, an urge to offer her a gift of words, however slight.

"We've both lived long enough to suffer the ending of many hopes. You're brave to take this step, Faridah. I really hope you find happiness. As for our past together, let's forgive ourselves for what we couldn't do then. Life is far too precious to waste on the past, my friend."

Tears fill her eyes. The sight of her tears causes me to suddenly break down. I weep loudly, without shame. We hold hands, feeling the subtle but vital throb of each other's life in our fingers. Her mouth quivers and slowly forms a smile of gratitude.

seventeen 脈

The next morning, I check out of Hotel 81 early. In the pre-dawn cool, I walk over to the dilapidated ruins of what used to be my grandfather's shop.

Where is the pulse of life? I ask myself.

Not here in the external ruins. Not anymore. But the pulse lives within me. If you touch me, if you know how to take pulses the way my Kong-Kong did, the way I've learned to do, lightly on the wrists, you will be able to know everything you need to know.

Words can deceive. But the body never lies.

There's one last thing I need to do before I leave the island. After checking in at the airport, I take a cab to the Changi Prison site at Upper Changi Road North, not too far from the airport. There remains a stretch of the original wall of the prison that housed about seventy-six thousand POWs—Allied soldiers and civilians imprisoned by the Japanese during the Second World War. I wonder how it was then, to be a member of the conquering army. Did the Japanese soldiers allow themselves to feel the horrors of war? Some of them must have.

I walk along the road, heading north, until I reach Changi Chapel and Museum. As I stand at the main entrance, I can see past the open iron gates into the chapel area inside. Just inside the entrance is the reception desk, where I'm given a map of the museum. I'm encouraged to start with the exhibition area ahead and to the left of the chapel, but I decide against it and walk straight into the chapel instead, heading down the aisle toward the altar. This chapel is a replica of the one originally built by the POWs. The aisle is flanked by twelve rows of wooden benches on either side, secured to the terracotta tiled floor. The chapel is built like a courtyard, open to the sky above. Like the courtyard that used to be behind Cosmic Pulse.

At the altar, built of a dark, rich tembusu wood, stands a cross fashioned out of spent artillery shells. Made by Sergeant Harry Ogden, it's perfectly proportioned, as far as I can tell, lean and balanced, with its two horizontal arms flowering into clover shapes.

I think of hands reaching out, hands transformed by the act of preparing for an embrace.

It's silent here. Shrubs on either side of the benches, a few cumulus clouds in an otherwise clear sky. *Have all the ghosts fled?* I wonder. I look around. There's a notice board festooned with messages written by visitors, messages in response to the Second World War. I am reminded that people of my parents' generation are the last witnesses of that war, and the Japanese occupation of Singapore.

I repeat the line from trigraph 53 of the Oracle quietly to myself, "Spirits of Heaven come down, releasing the entangled and freeing the imprisoned."

He wanted his father's love.

Just like me.

I hear Kong-Kong's voice, his stern tone summoning Hwi to pour out the brew. The sound of water splashing against the stone where clothes are being washed, the slosh and squeeze of water-laden clothes, the dripping of the tap faucet into the well. The radio is on, Hwi bent at the waist, peering down at the transistor radio, as if he could see the singer whose voice is filtering through.

There's a passion I can't talk about
Who will listen?
The one who knows my heart
Has left without a word

My lover surely hasn't changed
But why hasn't she written?
I've waited for so long

I walk down the narrow hallway, drawn by the sound of Mah-Mah's chips striking the table.

There she is, sitting and looking down at the chips. But when I enter, she glances at me and smiles a light, wistful smile.

"You see, granddaughter, what I mean?"

"Tell me, please."

"When time come, affairs complete. You wait all these years, and now is time you can see. You suffer bad things. Let go now."

I'm grateful for her presence, for being possessed by her wisdom. She was right in saying that the day would come when there would be release for the entangled.

I used to think that forgiving someone meant excusing his or her heinous acts. If that's the meaning of forgiveness, I can never forgive. I will never minimize the degree of suffering Papa caused me. Instead, I must release myself, redeem that inexplicable experience of inner freedom. Again and again. Abandon my investment in hating. This is what I think of when I utter under my breath, "Papa, I forgive you."

I can say it now. I turn away from the music of my childhood and leave the courtyard. The punishing harness has been loosened. I can feel the ropes falling off me, the strength returned to my limbs.

Neither he nor anyone else can bind my spirit. Once, because of what he did, my spirit fled to some cold, haunted place. I've found a way to summon it back. To let it dwell peaceably in my body.

ON THE plane, finally, after a ridiculously long layover at Hong Kong International Airport. I feel relieved that I'm on my way back to Toronto. Glad to have an aisle seat. There's an empty seat between me and the guy in the window seat, to my left.

I think of the first flight I took out of Singapore, with my parents, in 1979. It was a Philippine Airlines flight that stopped in Manila for over eight hours. All of the passengers were taken by shuttle to a nearby hotel to rest in complimentary rooms. Mum and Papa were impressed by the incredible extravagance of the airline, somehow not noticing that many of the passengers at the hotel were being inundated with pamphlets offering services.

We were all rather quiet during that time at the hotel. I remember going out on the balcony, wanting to get away from my parents, who were quite sullen. I looked out at the unfamiliar skyline. Thought about our brief respite in Manila. That it was a kind of purgatory. Even though we weren't Catholic.

Once we got on the second plane, though, things changed. Papa became very talkative. I had never seen him so animated. Mum looked a bit dazed, and her shoulders flinched every time Papa tapped her on the arm to talk. She hardly spoke, focusing instead on her Chinese novel. She occasionally looked up at the other passengers, wondering out loud how many of them were moving to Canada.

I had been nervous on that flight. Wondering what Toronto would be like, whether I could get used to the cold winters. It frightened me, being catapulted into the unknown, a new life that would bear no resemblance to my childhood.

How much I've changed. How much I've become accustomed to life in Toronto.

I tend to sleep very little on these long flights. After taking in a couple of movies, I decide to read. I take out *The Gay Science* from my backpack and switch on the overhead reading light. Many of the other passengers are sleeping.

I start to flip through the book. To my surprise, I find something taped inside the back cover. It's an envelope with my name on it.

Two sheets of paper in the envelope. The top sheet is dated August 10, the day I said goodbye to Faridah.

Dear Nat,

I've kept this letter all these years. Do you still have the scrap of paper I tore from it? I didn't feel ready then to give you the whole letter. I felt so awful about leaving you that I thought my words were useless. They certainly could not erase the harm that had been done. Selim knew about this letter. I'm sure that's why he told me to ask you for forgiveness. Why he said, and wrote, Godzilla's touch.

I could see from our visit this time how we've moved

beyond that place of being frozen in regret. This is the right time to give you this letter, filled with all the heart that I put into those few words. I never imagined—since losing our relationship—that I could be so open again.

I'm free now.

F.

My hands tremble as they take hold of the second letter. It is dated February 18, 1979. The bottom of the sheet is ripped. I recall the words on that scrap of paper: *Ps. You left this in my pencil case. Please don't lose this again, okay? And don't forget me, please.*

I had only those lines for all these years.

I start to read.

My beloved Natalie,
You promised me that you would never forget me. You promised.

I am sorry about what happened to you. You must accept why I had to leave you. I couldn't bear to risk you being punished any more by your father. I had to sacrifice, to protect you. And to get away from that angry man.

My parents love me so much. I owe them. Someday you'll understand.

So I'm married now. My life has changed. I've become responsible, a grown-up. No more foolishness.

But our years together were wonderful. I don't regret. Don't be angry forever. You see, my life may have changed, but I haven't. I will always love you.

That signature. That grand flourish, especially the "h" at the end, trailing off into the unknown.

I close my eyes and press my lips lightly together, savouring the warm energy that's overtaking me. It's a pleasure to be possessed like this. I surrender, without a trace of resistance.

Acknowledgements

This is a work of fiction. Names, characters, places and incidents either are products of the author's imagination or are used fictitiously. Any resemblance to actual events or locales or persons, living or dead, is entirely coincidental.

I would like to acknowledge the support of the Canada Council for the Arts toward the writing of this novel.

Many thanks to the following individuals for reading early versions of the manuscript: Dayaneetha De Silva, Joan Hollenberg, Daphne Marlatt, Joan Pillay, Carmen Rodriguez, Nancy Richler and my literary agent, Jessica Woollard.

My editor, Jane Warren, has a flair for tuning in to nuances. Her sensitive editorial input was invaluable in making this novel emotionally richer and more visceral. I am deeply grateful for her inspiration.

These people furnished essential technical or background information: Jenn Barrett, Ada Chan, Lawrence Chan, Fion Chou, Colin Koh, Eugene La'Brooy and Khuan Seow. Katherine Soucie found a copy of Ralph Sawyer's translation of *Ling Ch'i Ching* in a secondhand bookstore in Chicago and felt compelled to buy it for me. My mother taught me the Hakka saying that begins with: *Tzi zong tzi du . . .*

Thanks to the National Archives of Singapore for access to maps and historical information, and to staff at the National Library for help with past issues of *The Straits Times*.

Visits to the National Museum of Singapore and the Asian Civilizations Museum provided a fount of inspiration.

The layout of Cosmic Pulse was based on a herbal shop called An Tin Tong that existed in the same location on Joo Chiat Road in the 1960s and 70s. Details for the rooms above were inspired by a visit to the Baba and Nonya Heritage Museum in Malacca.

A thank you to Louise Francis-Smith and Canella Rupasingh for providing a hospitable retreat space during the summer of 2009.

My appreciation to Jason Sims for providing the Chinese character for "pulse" that adorns the beginning of each chapter.

A special note of thanks to Edward Gutierrez at Artistic Arts and Crafts in Vancouver's Chinatown; through conversations with him, I grew to appreciate the distinction between openness and vulnerability, which became a critical component of this novel.

And thanks to many others who inspired me unknowingly.

References

The epigraph is taken from R.D. Laing's *Knots* (London: Penguin, 1972), page 72. Reproduced by permission of Taylor and Francis Books UK.

"Mere existing ..." from *Tao Te Ching* is my version, based on Jonathan Star's translation (New York: Jeremy P. Tarcher/Putnam, 2001), passage 11.

The quotes "Faith is a myth and beliefs shift like mists on the shore" and "Life knows us not and we do not know life ..." are from a letter by Joseph Conrad to R. Cunningham Graham, in *Joseph Conrad, Life and Letters*, compiled by G. Jean-Aubry (London: William Heinemann Ltd, 1927), page 222.

The quote "It was the stillness of an implacable force brooding over an inscrutable intention" is from *Heart of Darkness* by Joseph Conrad (Oxford: Oxford University Press, 2003), page 48.

Tanka 35 is taken from *Tangled Hair* by Akiko Yosano, translated by Sanford Goldstein and Seishi Shinoda (Tokyo: Charles E. Tuttle Company, 1987).

Lines from "Desiderata" by Max Ehrmann are scattered throughout the book. Copyright 1927 by Max Ehrmann. Used by permission of Bell & Son Publishing, LLC. All rights reserved.

"What is well embraced cannot slip away" is a line paraphrased from Lao Tzu's *Tao Te Ching*, based on Jonathan

Star's translation (New York: Jeremy P. Tarcher/Putnam, 2001), passage 54.

The quote "My thoughts...premature tasting of things promised" is from *The Gay Science* by Friedrich Nietzsche, edited by Bernard Williams and translated by Josefine Nauckhoff (Cambridge: Cambridge University Press, 2001) , section 287, page 162.

My descriptions of trigraphs 51, 52 and 53 are paraphrased from Ralph Sawyer's translation of *Ling Ch'i Ching* (Cambridge: Westview Press/Perseus Books, 2004).

The tale behind the music of the Burdah comes from liner notes accompanying the CD *Selections from the Burdah* (Awakening Media, 2006).

Songs

"Undead, undead, undead" is from "Bela Lugosi's Dead" by Bauhaus.

"Hunt you to the ground they will, mannequins with kill appeal" is from "Diamond Dogs" by David Bowie.

"Love is the drug, got a hook on me ..." is from "Love is the Drug" by Roxy Music.

"Jesus loves me, this I know, for the Bible tells me so, little ones to Him belong ..." is from a hymn "Jesus Loves Me," lyrics by Anna B. Warner, music by William Bradbury.

"I'm waiting, waiting for you ..." is my translation of *"Deng Zhu Ni Hui Lai"* ("Waiting for You"), lyrics by Yan Kuan, music by Chen Rui Zhen.

"This is the dawning of the Age of Aquarius"; "and love will steer the stars"; and "When the moon is in the seventh house" are from "Aquarius," from the musical *Hair*, lyrics by James Rado and Gerome Ragni, music by Galt MacDermot.

"Run to me whenever you're lonely . . ." is from "Run to Me" by the Bee Gees.

"My love for you, unrequited . . ." is my translation of *"De Bu Dao Ni De Ai Qing"* ("Unrequited Love"), lyrics by Lu Li, music by Yao Min.

"Wang bu liao, wang bu liao ni de ai . . ." is from *"Wang Bu Liao"* ("Can't Forget"), music and lyrics by Wang Fu Ling. I provided the English translation.

"There's a passion I can't talk about . . ." is my translation of *"Wo You Yi Duan Qing"* ("I Have a Tale of Passion"), lyrics by Mei Meng, music by Xin Yi.

Movies

The original Japanese movie *Gojira* was released by Toho Studios in 1954. The American version was *Godzilla, King of the Monsters*, released in 1956.

Sympathy for Lady Vengeance (2005) is a thriller by South Korean filmmaker Park Chan-wook.

Bu Liao Qing (Love Without End) was released by Shaw Brothers in 1961. Lin Dai was named Best Actress at the Asian Film Festival for her performance as the doomed songstress.

Sources

Dechar, Lorie Eve. *Five Spirits*. New York: Chiron Publications/Lantern Books, 2006.

Heidhues, Mary Somers. *Southeast Asia: A Concise History*. London: Thames & Hudson, 2000.

McNamara, Sheila. *Traditional Chinese Medicine*. New York: Basic Books/HarperCollins, 1996.

Midori. *The Seductive Art of Japanese Bondage*. Oakland, CA: Greenery Press, 2001.

Yin Yang House: http://www.yinyanghouse.com/

photo by Jason Sims

Lydia Kwa grew up in Singapore but has called Canada home since 1980. She has published poetry (*The Colours of Heroines*, Women's Press, 1994) and two previous novels *This Place Called Absence* (Turnstone Press, 2000) and *The Walking Boy* (Key Porter Books, 2005). She lives and works in Vancouver as a writer and psychologist. Please see www.lydiakwa.com for more on the author.